"You aren't mad at me for turning you over to Collingswood?"

"Mad? Not really. It surprised me, I have to admit." She pressed a bit closer. He felt her hot breath against his throat and the beating of her heart through her breast and thin dress. "It is almost impossible to find a man with such integrity."

"I worked for the railroad. I gave my word."

"That's what makes you so different. Too many men see a promise made as a sometime thing."

"I don't work for the railroad any longer."

"No duty to either Mr. Collingswood or the Central California Railroad," she said. "You aren't beholden to them anymore?"

Slocum put his hands around her slender waist. He felt the heat from her body. It matched his own.

"Not a bit. What about you? You still have your job."

"I never promised to find the silver or make sure it ended up in the bank vault owned by the railroad."

"Do tell," he said. He pulled her closer until they both gasped for breath.

"I want someone who can give me his word, and I'll know he can keep it."

"Unlike Jackson."

"We can work together."

"Can I trust your word?"

"We can spit in our palms and shake on it," she said.

"That's not good enough. I know you're a crook."

"What more can I do to show you I can keep my word if we agree to be partners? What can seal the contract?"

Slocum caught his breath as her hand wormed its way between their tightly pressed bodies and began inching down from his chest to his belly, and then even lower until she gripped the growing bulge at his crotch.

JAKE LOGAN

SLOCUM'S SILVER BURDEN

JOVE BOOKS, NEW YORK

THE BERKLEY PUBLISHING GROUP
Published by the Penguin Group
Penguin Group (USA) LLC
375 Hudson Street, New York, New York 10014

USA • Canada • UK • Ireland • Australia • New Zealand • India • South Africa • China

penguin.com

A Penguin Random House Company

SLOCUM'S SILVER BURDEN

A Jove Book / published by arrangement with the author

For information, address: The Berkley Publishing Group,
a division of Penguin Group (USA) LLC,
375 Hudson Street, New York, New York 10014.

ISBN: 978-0-515-15493-1

PUBLISHING HISTORY
Jove mass-market edition / December 2014

PRINTED IN THE UNITED STATES OF AMERICA

10 9 8 7 6 5 4 3 2 1

Cover illustration by Sergio Giovine.

Prologue

"You lied to us, Jackson." The tall, rangy, unnaturally ashen man dressed like a placer miner hefted his rifle and moved it in his partner's direction.

"Shut yer tater trap, Drury." The second of the four men waiting nervously beside their horses put down his field glasses and glared at the former miner. "Jack's not the kind to lie 'bout something this big."

"Thanks for the vote of confidence," Jackson said. He hitched up his gun belt as he glared at Drury. The man had been the weak link ever since he'd recruited him from the saloon along San Francisco's treacherous Barbary Coast. If he hadn't come along with this job, Drury would have been shanghaied for sure, all pale and shaking the way he did.

The truth was he had saved all three of his partners from different fates far worse than waiting for a train that never seemed to be on schedule. Drury had a bad drinking problem and made it worse chasing the dragon in opium dens along Dupont Gai. A stint on a China clipper's two-year trip to the Orient as a deckhand might have improved his lot in

1

life, but nothing would change his sour disposition or volatile anger.

As much of a naysayer as Drury was, their lookout was worse in his way. Baldy Wilson was a suck-up, and nothing Jackson said was ever wrong. When they had started planning this robbery, all Baldy wanted to do was sit around, drink, and tell everyone how great it would be to get rich, and how it was all Henry Jackson's brilliance that was going to dump a ton of money into their laps. Jackson wanted Baldy to shut up and find out the information they needed from the railroad agent in Oakland, but Baldy had proven untrustworthy. He was as likely to spill his guts about the robbery to the station agent, boasting of the haul they would make, as he was to find the information about grades and engine speeds.

For that, Jackson had reluctantly relied on the fourth man in their small gang. Pierre Montague gave him a queasy stomach. The man's dark eyes never blinked, always watched, and no emotion showed through. If Jackson had to pick one of the gang most likely to shoot him in the back and take his share, Montague was it. In spite of the man's name, he wasn't French or even Acadian. Rumor had it that his ma had no idea who his pa was, but she wanted it to be a dashing Frenchie she had met in New Orleans. Montague had been born aboard a paddle wheeler on the river, churning hard for Natchez, a father or even a namesake nowhere to be found.

Other gossip claimed that Montague had popped out of his mama's womb and immediately kicked her into the muddy river to drown. Jackson doubted it, but given what he knew about the man, he understood how such a story could arise. Still, Montague had a way with the ladies and had romanced that general store owner's wife into giving them supplies they could never have paid for. Not having to steal the gear and victuals made them just a tad more invisible.

After they got around to robbing the train, they had to vanish fast. While sweet-talking his own lady, he'd learned that the Central California Railroad had a low tolerance for getting robbed. There was even talk that the vice president in charge of this line from Sacramento to Oakland had personally tracked down two inept robbers by himself, skinned them alive, and then tossed them into San Francisco Bay, where the saltwater brined them up for the sharks to eat. Jackson had never caught sight of David Collingswood, but he had quite a reputation. In spite of what Tamara said about him being a pussycat, the reputation was a powerful one, though it looked as if easy living in San Francisco had turned the man soft and careless.

"You sure this train's the one, Jackson?"

He glared at Drury.

"Why don't you just step up on that swayback nag of yours and leave if you got doubts? Splitting the money four ways is better than five."

"Yeah, Drury. Leave. It's better 'n listening to you bad-mouth Jack the way you do," piped up Baldy. "If it weren't for him, we wouldn't have any notion at all 'bout what the train's carryin'. He got the information straight from the horse's mouth."

"Yeah," Drury said, sneering. "That bitch of his looks more like a horse than a woman. Might be 'cuz all she says to him is *nay*."

Jackson considered his options. Drury was egging him into a fight for some reason. It might be nothing more than a nasty disposition, or he might be angling to get acknowledgment from the others that he was the gang leader. Jackson looked at Montague and not Baldy for support. Baldy would follow whoever called himself the boss. Montague had to back any play against Drury.

He moved so Montague stood behind Drury. Only then did he square off, push back his coat to rest his hand on the side of his holster. If Drury made the slightest twitch, he'd be a dead man. Jackson had put up with the constant bitching long enough. Insulting Tamara bothered him less than the way Drury made a play to take over.

"We do all the dirty work and risk our necks, and she gets an equal share," Drury said. "Where's the justice in that?"

"Without her telling us about this shipment out of Virginia City, we'd still be sitting in a saloon and getting drunk, bragging on what we've done, not how rich we can be. How rich we *will* be."

Drury pushed back his coat, ready to throw down. At that instant Baldy cried out, "There's the train! I see the smoke from its stack. We got to get down there, Jack. We don't want to miss our chance."

"This is the steepest grade before the train gets over the hills and heads down into Oakland," Jackson said.

"I don't care if it's highballin'. I can rob it blindfolded."

"We got to ride. Now," said Montague.

Jackson saw that Montague held his rifle so a single round from it would shatter Drury's spine. He wished Montague would pull the trigger. Three of them could rob the train just fine.

"Might be you got it right for a change, Jackson," said Drury. "Let's find out if there's so much as a silver dollar on the train."

"I'm seein' a whale of a lot of trouble," Baldy said, his eyes pressed to the lenses of his field glasses. "There must be a half-dozen armed guards on top of the train. Never seen 'em ride like that before."

"The grade's close to three percent. That'll shake them up," Jackson said, shoving Drury out of the way. The back of his neck prickled as he waited for the man to back-shoot him. When the expected bullet never came, he said, "We know what to do. Don't worry about the guards. Montague will take them out. Right, Pierre?"

All he got from the man was a grunt. Montague moved

forward, flopped on his belly, and levered in a round. He took a slow breath, let it out, and fired. Jackson saw a guard on the roof of the mail car jerk about and fall off the train, hidden by the cars. On the far side was a steep cliff. If the guard tumbled down that, he was a goner, even if Montague's shot had only wounded him.

Montague wasted no more time. He fired slowly, accurately, taking out a guard with every shot. Where the man had learned to shoot like that hardly mattered to Jackson. Not riding into the gun barrels of a half-dozen railroad guards did. He galloped hard. The engineer had twigged to the robbery and had his fireman working overtime to feed the boiler. Jackson had asked around enough to know the engineer had a better chance of blowing a valve than he did of gaining speed on this steep slope.

Keeping low, he ducked a few rounds making their way toward him. Montague proved himself to be a real sharpshooter. No guard got a second shot at any of the men galloping for the mail car. When the sniper's rifle fell silent, Jackson knew they were almost rich. All that separated them from a couple hundred dollars each in silver was a thin wooden door.

"Open up and we won't hurt you," Jackson called out, trotting alongside the slow-moving train. "We just want what you're carryin'."

A shrill scream like that of a frightened woman came from inside the car. Then holes began appearing in the door as the mail clerk foolishly fired through the wood.

Jackson counted. At six, he motioned to Drury and Baldy. They shot off the lock on the door and swung it back along its track as Jackson rode up and shoved his six-gun into the frightened clerk's face. The man was hardly out of his teens. From the look of his face, he had either a bad case of acne or a mild one of smallpox. Each pimple had turned fiery red in his fear. The man's eyes were big and wide, and a bit of drool worked from the corner of his mouth.

"Drop it or I'll drop you."

The clerk looked down to see how he fumbled with the six-shooter in his hands. He was trying to load it without opening the gate. All the shells had tumbled to the floor and rattled about as the train ground to a halt. Montague was still doing his job, getting the drop on the engineer and his brakeman.

"Don't kill me!"

"Get the coupling," Jackson bellowed. The words had barely left his lips when the metallic grinding told him Montague had done his part again.

The locomotive pulled a lighter load now and shot forward, hit the top of the grade, and vanished over the summit in seconds. What he hadn't counted on was the mail car and caboose, once free of the rest of the train, rolling back downhill. For a moment, the mail car stood still, then began the inexorable trip back down the steep hill it had just scaled.

"Get on the car. Set the brake! It's rollin' away from us!"

Jackson's order accomplished nothing. Both Drury and Baldy were on the ground. Montague had dismounted to work at the coupler. He let out a loud curse and started riding after the escaping cars. Jackson rode close enough to see the metal rungs driven into the front of the car. He had done some bulldogging in his day and figured this couldn't be much different. He judged the distance, got his toes square in the stirrups, and launched himself.

He misjudged the distance and crashed into the car, sliding down the rough wall. Frantically, he grabbed for the ladder. At the last possible instant his fingers curled around a rung. The rusted metal cut into his hand, but he hung on grimly. With a powerful jerk, he swung himself around. His toes dragged along the ties and cinders in the roadbed. Every time he hit one of the ties, he was almost jolted from his grip. Through sheer will, he got one foot under him and kicked hard. This sent him up high enough to grab a second rung. From there he pulled himself up far enough to secure a foothold. In seconds he scrambled up to the roof and found the handle for the car's handbrake.

His back screaming in protest, he fought to turn the rusted wheel. He dug his toes into the roof, got purchase, and finally felt the brake turn a fraction of an inch. Another, another, and then it broke free. He almost pitched from the roof as the wheel made a half circuit. Then he felt the metal grinding down into the wheels. Tortured hot metal smells rose, and a shower of sparks from the wheels shot back toward his three partners. They veered away to keep from being set on fire.

Then he heard cries of fear from the caboose. The three men riding in it jumped, hit the ground with loud thuds, and lay still. A second later the mail clerk shot from the door beneath Jackson's feet. His scream continued for quite a spell. He had picked the wrong spot to escape and had jumped out over a fifty-foot drop into a rocky ravine. Jackson tried to see what happened to the clerk, then decided his stomach wasn't up for seeing guts and brains smeared all over the hillside.

He pushed harder on the brake to slow the deadly downhill slide. The mail car came to a grating halt, but it was still coupled to the caboose. Jackson barely jumped before the caboose tipped over and derailed, taking part of the mail car with it. From the far side of the railroad tracks, Jackson sat up and stared. It looked as if a giant hand had reached down from the sky and plucked away the back half of the mail car, leaving the front still on its wheels on the tracks.

"You all right, Jack?"

"Yeah, I am." Jackson got to his feet. Baldy handed down his reins. "That was one hell of a wreck."

"We mighta lost the vault over the cliff," grumbled Drury. "You could have kept everything all upright on the tracks."

Jackson touched the six-shooter in his holster. A single shot would be all it took, but he saw that Drury was ready for such a move. Even with all the money from the mail car waiting for them, he stirred up trouble. His dark eyes looked like burning coals set in a pasty white face.

Montague rode up, then jumped into what remained of the car. By the time Jackson reached the torn-off rear of the car, Montague had opened the vault.

"How'd you do that so fast?" Jackson hopped up. "I reckoned it would take us an hour to open the vault if the mail clerk wouldn't do it." He snorted. There wasn't any way the mail clerk would open anything, including his own coffin lid.

"It was smashed open." Montague's voice was small, tiny, timid.

"What's wrong? The vault empty?" Jackson pushed past his partner and stared. "Oh, sweet Jesus."

Drury and Baldy joined them. They all stared at the take, then at each other.

"There must be a ton of silver there," Baldy finally said. "We're rich. Dammit, we're rich!"

He began dancing around, whooping, hollering, and swatting his floppy-brimmed hat against his thigh.

"Why're you so quiet? Both of you?" Drury went to the safe and ran his fingers over the silver bars stacked inside. "I know metal. This is the real thing. What's wrong?"

"There must be a couple hundred bars there," Montague said. "How are we gonna take it all?"

Jackson sucked in his breath. This was an embarrassment of riches he had never expected. From what Tamara had said, the shipment would be good, maybe a few hundred dollars. He had hoped for a thousand. But this?

"What's your problem? We struck the mother lode," Drury said, happy for the first time.

"You got a pack mule with you? No? Well, neither do I. None of us expected to be starin' at so much silver."

"Must be three, four hundred pounds," Montague said,

moving the bars and judging the weight, then doing a quick count in the huge vault. "More like half a ton."

"So?"

"So how are you going to strap on an extra two-hundred pounds of silver bars and ride your horse, too? The horse'd die under you before we reached the bottom of the hill."

"We can take what we can carry," Montague said. Then he and Jackson locked eyes.

The same thought went through both their heads. Jackson wasn't going to leave so much as a speck of silver dust behind. Montague had the same feeling. They had risked their lives for this and wanted to get as much as possible.

But his horse barely carried him at a hundred and twenty pounds. More than doubling the weight would make it bow-legged within a mile and dead from strain in two.

"We can't leave it. That's just not . . . right." Montague sucked in a deep breath. "What are we gonna do, Jackson?"

"I don't know."

"You said we ain't got much time. The engineer's gonna find a telegraph wire alongside the tracks and send a message."

It was a risky job climbing a telegraph pole and hooking a loop around the strung telegraph wire. Somehow this made a connection so a man who knew Morse code could send along a warning. Jackson had tried to find out if anyone on this train knew the technique. Even if they did, they had to send a coded message. As malingerers, telegraph operators were about the worst. They had a valuable skill and seldom got fired, no matter how bad their misdeeds. Even if the operator received a message about the train robbery, it might be a spell before the information got passed along to the law.

Or it might be in the hands of a sheriff right now.

Jackson eyed the mountain of silver bars. A dozen ideas flashed through his head.

"We can toss the bars over the cliff and come get them later," he said.

"Like hell I will," said Drury. "What's to keep you from getting there first and taking it all?"

"Or you?" said Baldy. "You and a dozen pack mules would be more 'n up to the chore."

"You haven't looked over the side," Montague said. "That's a sheer drop. You got any notion how to reach the bottom?"

"I don't, and even if we figured it out, we couldn't heave the silver out far enough to get all the way down. There'd be silver strewn the whole way down for the railroad dicks to recover."

"We don't have much choice, not if we want to take it all."

"What's your plan, Jack?" Baldy looked eagerly at his boss.

"We load our horses with as much as they'll carry, get down the mountainside, then split up. Hide the silver wherever you like or try to make it away with your horse loaded down. Whatever we do, we scatter to the four winds."

"You want to know where I'm gonna hide my share?" Baldy frowned as the other three glared at him.

"Don't tell us," Jackson said. "Keep it a secret. If one of us gets caught, the other three's stashes will be safe."

"What if all of us are caught?" Drury thrust out his chin belligerently.

"Then you'll get a chance to shoot it out, like you been itchin' to do. Or we can all watch one another get our necks stretched. Men died in this robbery."

"We didn't kill 'em," protested Baldy. "They jumped on their own. 'Cept the ones Montague shot."

"I'm not going to argue that with a jury," Montague said. He bent to the task of moving the silver bars to the edge of the car.

Jackson saw him fetch his horse and begin working to use the saddle blanket and his duster as a way of keeping the metal bars on his horse's back. Montague had started back for another load when Jackson joined in. He said nothing as Drury and Baldy began moving their share of the silver, too.

Every second dragged like an eternity. He expected the sound of a steam whistle on a train bringing the railroad bulls.

"I can't load the rest," complained Drury. "My horse's belly's about draggin' on the ground."

Jackson tugged on his horse's reins.

"Do what you want."

"See you in hell, Jackson!" Drury shouted, then returned to the final few silver bars still in the vault.

Jackson saw that Montague and Baldy were already ahead of him, heading down the hillside. He reached the level spot where a couple canyons branched away. Montague had already disappeared down one. With luck he wouldn't follow the one the other man already had. Or he could keep moving and hunt for a different place to go, but this looked chancy. Baldy had stopped and eyed him, as if waiting for orders.

Deciding it was for the best, Jackson motioned for Baldy Wilson to take one of the routes away. He kept going for another couple miles, his horse increasingly tired by the heavy load. Jackson tried to guess how much he had piled on. It might be as much as two hundred pounds. He thought he had three thousand dollars' worth of silver bullion bouncing along a couple feet away.

His anxiety at being found by the railroad bulls finally wore him down. He found a railroad way marker, then cut across country to find a spot to bury the silver for later retrieval. As he went, he drew a map for Tamara. He didn't mind splitting his take in half with her since what remained was ten times what he'd expected to steal.

It was almost dawn when he found a decent spot to begin burying his treasure. Jackson slept until noon, had a meal, finished his map, and then cut across country away from the railroad tracks to find a way to San Francisco that wouldn't expose him to what might be the biggest posse in the history of California hunting for the silver.

He didn't know for certain if the engineer had even sent out the news of the theft, but it made him feel better thinking he was the biggest, baddest outlaw ever.

1

John Slocum took a step back, brought up his fists, and took the measure of his opponent. The man moved like a bull and looked like one, only uglier. His eyebrows grew together, giving him a fierce look when he squinted. His dull brown eyes darted about, not studying Slocum as much as the men gathered in a ring around them. When Slocum saw the man's interest was more on the bets being placed than the fight, he moved fast. With two quick steps, he shoved his shoulder into the bull man's, knocking him off balance. As the man tried to regain his feet, Slocum launched a short punch to the heart that traveled less than six inches.

He felt the impact all the way up to his shoulder. Slocum swung his left hand up and over the man's flailing arm and crushed his fist into an exposed temple. Like a bull shot behind the ear, the man's eyes rolled up in his head as he crumpled to the dock, where he lay twitching feebly.

The crowd had been cheering and jeering. It went utterly silent now that the favorite had been vanquished so quickly.

"You took out Bully Boy with one punch," the man

holding the bets said in a choked voice. "Ain't nobody ever done that before."

"I hit him twice," Slocum said. He faced the man and plucked the greenbacks from his fist.

"Wait, you can't—" The man swallowed hard and went pale under the caked grime that had turned his face almost black from weeks of not bathing.

Slocum counted out the money he had been promised and held up the rest for the crowd to see.

"Who bet on me?"

For a long second no one said anything. Then one man in the back held up his hand. Or what remained of it. Three fingers were missing, leaving only his index finger and thumb.

"Come get your winnings." Slocum waited for the man to push through the crowd. Grumbles were muffled but grew when Slocum handed all the money to the lone winner.

"First time I was smart 'nuff to back a winner," the man said, taking the money between thumb and forefinger. He stuffed the money into his pocket.

Slocum waited for the trouble to start, but having the man beside him changed the way the crowd acted. Still grumbling, they slowly drifted away until only the gambler and the winner remained.

"You owe me. I set up the fight," said the gambler.

"You owe Bully Boy," the man beside Slocum said. "This the first time he's been beat, ain't it?"

"Me and you, we can make a boatload of money," the gambler said to Slocum. "Lose the next one and set up for a rematch and we'll clean the lot of them out of every dime they've ever earned or stole."

"Not interested," Slocum said, turning away.

"Hell, you could get rich. What's the matter with you? Don't you like the idea of winnin' so much money?"

The gambler saw Slocum's expression and snorted in disgust, then went to the fallen fighter and kicked him to see if he got any response. The fighter moaned, and his eyelids flickered. He was still out like a light. Then the gambler bent, grabbed Bully Boy by the shoulders, and dragged him to the edge of the dock. Panting from the exertion, the gambler tipped his fighter over the edge to land with a loud splash ten feet below in San Francisco Bay.

"Why'd you do that?" Slocum asked.

"He lost. He ain't no good to me now. I hope he gets et by the fishes."

The man beside Slocum laughed.

"More likely, he'll pizzen the fishes."

The gambler started to ask Slocum once more to fight for him, then saw the answer etched in every line on his angular face. Without looking back, the gambler stalked off, muttering to himself about having to go back to three-card monte to make a living.

"You do handle yourself with aplomb," said the two-fingered man.

"What happened to your hand? You a fighter?" Slocum asked.

The man held up his finger and thumb and wiggled them.

"Bein' a sailor's a right dangerous way to live. I got all caught up in rigging and fell off a slippery spar. Part of me hit the deck. Some of me stayed aloft in the rigging."

The man studied Slocum hard, then said, "I ain't up for a job I heard about, but you got the look of a man who can handle himself if I put in a good recommendation."

Slocum shrugged. He had hunted for work along the Embarcadero for a week and hadn't turned up anything. Shipping was light at the moment, and the dockworkers who had jobs protected them jealously. The foremen weren't inclined to take on new workers when they couldn't keep their old hands busy.

He had come to San Francisco on a horse that had died under him as he rode into Portsmouth Square. His fortune had gone downhill from there. The dives along the Barbary

Coast were death traps he had wisely avoided. Nobody unknown to the barkeeps or owners escaped without getting their gut filled with Mickey Finns before being spirited off to the ships anchored in the harbor. There might not have been much call for dockhands but the ships' captains had an insatiable appetite for new deckhands. Once aboard a ship, the shanghaied landlubber found himself impressed into service for two years or better. Once the drug from the drink wore off, a shanghaied sailor had a long walk back.

Rather than drink there, Slocum had stayed closer to the center of town. He had passed by Russian Hill once, had taken a look at the Union Club on Nob Hill, and watched the fancy carriages with their well-dressed men and beautiful women decked out in jewels rattle by. Footsore and down to his last nickel, Slocum had considered a robbery to get back on his feet. Not a one of the carriages didn't also have a pair of armed guards riding close behind.

Slocum had eventually come to the docks and gotten into the fight. The gambler had taken one look at his rangy, emaciated frame and had thought he would be an easy opponent for Bully Boy. For ten dollars, Slocum would have let himself get pounded on, but a glance at the other fighter had revealed more muscle than skill.

"My name's Underwood. Julius Underwood, late of Boston and other points north in New England."

"You're a ways from home."

"You are, too. I got me a good ear for accents. South Carolina? No, wait, Georgia."

"Why'd you bet on me?"

"Odds. The longer the odds, the bigger the payoff."

Slocum laughed at this. Underwood had no confidence in his abilities but put money down on all the longshots in the hope of getting rich quick. Slocum wasn't averse to making such a bet himself, but he needed more than a ghost of a chance to win. He had to see some talent, some hope, have a tad of conviction to place such a wager.

Had Underwood seen that in him, in spite of what the two-fingered sailor said?

"Wish I had money to bet on myself." Slocum touched the ten dollars in his vest pocket. "Time for me to get some food."

"I'll buy you a drink if you'll listen to me for five minutes."

Underwood was sturdy, but he had other injuries besides his hand from the way he dragged his left leg just a mite. Additional evidence came in his cough, deep and rattling. When he spat, bloody phlegm hit the street.

"You're the one who looks like he needs a drink."

"That I do. Good thing my employer don't mind if I knock back a shot or two while I'm workin."

"You're on the job?"

"You can say that. You're no sailor or stevedore. I been on or by the sea long enough to know that. No, I make you out to be a cowboy. A wrangler down on his luck." Underwood peered around to Slocum's left hip, where his Colt Navy was slung. "Or maybe from the way you fight and the worn grips on that hogleg, you might be a shootist."

"Not that. If you're looking for someone to kill for you, keep hunting."

"Not that, no, sir, not that. My job's to recruit, it's true, but for a real job. A good one with the railroad."

"I've done some work on a railroad, but not around here. Not in California."

"We got plenny of them Celestials to do the hard work. You ever see any of 'em at work? I do declare, they're scrawny little things, and they do the work of three men. Each of 'em, eatin' nothin' more 'n a bowl of rice a day. I was up in the hills when they was goin' across Las Trampas Ridge in the early days. They got a way of swingin' down sheer rock walls in baskets and chiselin' out a roadbed. Damnedest thing you ever did see."

"I haven't heard of any railroads being built around here."

"Nope, you wouldn't. We got all the track laid we need

for another fifty years. It's not that kind of job I'm recruitin' for."

They went into a restaurant a few blocks from the Embarcadero on Market Street that didn't look as if it would poison them. Slocum settled down and realized how tired he was. Walking wore on him. He wished the horse hadn't upped and died. If it had been necessary, Slocum could have sold the old nag for a few dollars to keep him going. More likely he would have turned back south and headed for San Diego. Prospects there had to be better than here. Better yet, San Diego was warm while San Francisco was cold and wet all the time.

Slocum ordered, drank a cup of the bitter coffee, and felt better for it. By the time the pork chops with greens and boiled potatoes arrived, Underwood had begun his sales pitch. Slocum had heard the buskers around Portsmouth Square and had learned to ignore their songs and lectures. He ate with grim determination to fill his belly, and only when he'd finished some peach cobbler did he settle back and let the other man's words work their way into his head.

"I'm what you call a recruiter for the Central California Railroad."

"Never heard of it," Slocum said.

"Don't matter. It's a good line, short line for the most part, working out of the goldfields in Virginia City and comin' 'cross the Sierras to Sacramento 'fore chuggin' on into the Oakland depot."

"Across the Bay?"

"The ferry service is good 'twixt here and Berkeley. Most of the railroad owners prefer to have offices in San Francisco, though heaven alone knows most of 'em never seen their depots other than to step into a Pullman car. But Mr. Collingswood's different. He's worked 'bout every possible job on the line. Worked his way up from haulin' water fer the coolies to foreman and then to director."

"He's a director of the Central California Railroad?"

"Director and a vice president in charge of special freight. Or somethin' like that."

"He needs men to load the cars?" Slocum considered this a moment. He had tried to find work moving crates on the waterfront. Doing the same only on and off railroad cars wasn't much different. "I don't cotton much to the salt air. Workin' across the Bay in the hills would suit me just fine."

"Ain't that kind of job. Mr. Collingswood, he needs men what can handle themselves. Like you."

"Bodyguard? Or to break up union fights? That's not for me." Slocum stood and stared at the old salt. Underwood started to protest. "Thanks for betting on me."

"Wait, mister. I ain't bought you that drink. Ole Julius Underwood never goes back on his word." ·

"Next time," Slocum said. He wanted liquor without knockout drops in it, and he suspected Underwood wasn't above trying the shanghaiers' trick to recruit for the Central California Railroad.

Slocum paid for his meal and stepped out into the cool San Francisco air. A breeze off the Bay carried a chill to it that Slocum didn't appreciate. He turned up his coat collar and started down Market Street. He hadn't gone ten paces when he heard the sharp click-click of hobnailed boots hitting the pavement behind him. He reached over and slipped the leather thong off the hammer of his Colt and started to see who was rushing up from behind.

"You son of a bitch!"

The curse accompanied a hard fist aimed at his face. Slocum ducked as the mallet of bone and flesh slipped past him so close he felt the wind of its passage. He was off balance and couldn't strike back or get his pistol free. Two quick steps into the street almost got him run over by a carriage. Dodging the horse and the driver's whip and cussing, he faced Bully Boy. The giant of a man had swung so hard it had thrown him to his knees. He clambered back to his feet and stood with his fists cocked and ready for a fight.

Slocum doubted he would be as lucky this time. There weren't any bettors to distract Bully Boy.

"I'm gonna turn your face to mush, you piece of bilge."

"You're dumber than you look if you fight for nothing."

"What do you mean?"

"You're not getting paid to get laid out again," Slocum said. "The only difference this time is I'm not rolling you into the Bay. You go down now, you'll stay down."

"Andy Yulin ain't gonna pay me no more 'cuz you whupped up on me."

"Yulin? The gambler?" Slocum had no interest in the man's name. All he wanted was to buy time. Bully Boy might settle down. "I'll buy you a shot of whiskey to show there's no hard feelings."

This had the effect Slocum expected. Bully Boy roared in rage and charged, his arms going wide to scoop Slocum up in a bear hug. A quick twist sent Slocum's left arm into Bully Boy's right, letting him spin past. He used his right fist like a hammer on the back of the giant's neck. His hand bounced off like raindrops from a slicker. The man's bull namesake had nothing on him for strength and pure mean.

"Sucker punch me, will you?" Bully Boy shook his head, then attacked.

Slocum's straight punch to the prominent nose broke cartilage and caused a fountain of blood. Bully Boy was so het up he never noticed and kept coming, knocking Slocum back. Heavy blows landed on Slocum's upturned forearms until he felt the strength ebbing from the beating he took. Any one of those punches would have laid him out in the street if it had reached his head or body. He began to understand how lucky he had been in their first fight.

He managed to curl a fist around in a haymaker to land in Bully Boy's breadbasket. This slowed the man but didn't stop him. Slocum danced back and reached for his six-shooter. That proved to be a mistake. He was caught up in the man's ponderous arms, his hand trapped between them and his six-shooter still in its holster.

Bully Boy turned red in the face as he strained to break Slocum's back. He heaved and got him off his feet and swung him around like a rag doll.

"You're gonna pay fer puttin' me on the outs with Yulin. I'm gonna take your head to him in a peach basket and get my job back."

Slocum began to black out. Every exhalation brought him closer to death. He couldn't suck in more air because of the powerful arms around his body. As the air was crushed from him, he pulled back the Colt's hammer and let it drop without coming to full cock.

The muffled report brought an immediate response. Bully Boy tightened his grip even more, then released Slocum. He looked down at his thigh. Blood from his nose already smeared his clothes, but the new source of blood spoke of a more serious injury.

"I can't feel my leg. It . . . it's all cold," Bully Boy said, sitting down hard. He stared at his leg.

Slocum had shot through an artery. The man's life pumped out into the gutter. In seconds, Bully Boy slumped over. For all anyone knew, he was another drunk passed out on the curb.

Gasping hard, letting air painfully fill his lungs again, Slocum considered what to do. The brief fight hadn't brought any attention from incurious passersby. But two policemen walked their beat down the street and came in his direction. Fighting was one thing, but murder was another. It had been self-defense, but Slocum had heard about the San Francisco lawmen. There wasn't a crime they wouldn't overlook—for a price. If that price wasn't paid and a felon was dragged off to the jailhouse on Bryant Street, like as not he was never seen again. Not alive. Slocum would have been better served to let Yulin roll him into the Bay to fight off the sharks.

He might cut down both policemen, but that raised new

problems. Where he stood on Market wasn't far from the police station on Sixth. Gunshots would bring a small army of cops running. Slocum looked down at the man he had shot, then turned and started to walk away.

He froze when the two policemen yelled out for him to stop. He had scant chance of talking his way out of the killing. Slocum started to run but found his feet kicking at empty air. A powerful arm had circled his shoulders and lifted him off the pavement.

He was a goner for sure.

2

"Don't struggle," came the harsh whisper in his ear.

Slocum tensed, then relaxed and tried to wiggle free so he could whip out his six-gun and get away. He stopped fighting when he saw the hand holding him was missing three fingers.

"Let me go, Underwood. The police are—"

"They're too drunk to notice anything," Underwood said. He kept his strong grip on Slocum and steered him into the middle of Market Street. Drivers shouted and one carriage tried to run them down. The driver swung a whip around but missed them by a country mile, which set off a new round of swearing as the carriage rattled past.

With an agility that had to have been learned walking on a saltwater-slippery spar, Underwood avoided the traffic and kept Slocum moving along to the opposite side of the street.

"Keep that iron in its place." Underwood spun Slocum around so he could look back across the busy street at Bully Boy's body slumped over. "Do you see them fools tryin' to figure out why a man's passed out at their feet? Not a bit of it. They don't care, 'less they think to rob him."

One policeman knelt and the other used his club to hasten onlookers along with strategically placed taps. The kneeling cop expertly emptied Bully Boy's pockets, found little, then stood and kicked the dead man.

"He feels cheated that the man he was robbin' was broke. Never occurred to him that Bully Boy was dead. And it wouldn't matter one whit to him if he figgered it out."

The two cops walked on, never looking back at the corpse.

"Thanks. I was feeling guilty over killing him and would have shot both policemen."

"That would have brought the wrath of God down on you. Or at least the wrath of James Otis."

"Who's that?"

"The mayor of this fine city. But maybe he isn't carin' so much at the moment. Heard the rumor he's afflicted with cholera and doin' poorly."

"Why were you following me?"

"It's like this, mister. You know my name, but I don't know yours." Underwood looked sharply at Slocum. He might be lacking fingers but his gaze was intent. Nothing dulled his bright blue eyes.

Slocum gave his name but nothing more. He had wanted posters that had followed him for all the years after the end of the war for killing a carpetbagger judge who had tried to steal Slocum's Stand, the farm that had been in his family for generations. He had left the judge and his hired gunman in graves down by the springhouse, ridden away, and never looked back to see who was catching up with him. Since then, he hadn't lived a perfect life. More than once he had sampled the outlaw life. Whatever it took to keep body and soul together, he did. He preferred legal jobs, but he wasn't inclined to be dragged into a crime by someone he didn't know.

"I want to offer you a job."

Slocum had anticipated this.

"I already told you that I'm not a killer for hire."

"But takin' a man's life in self-defense doesn't bother you overly, does it? You're not sheddin' tears over Bully Boy."

"He would have killed me," Slocum said simply.

"You think them police did the right thing? Robbin' a dead man?"

Slocum shrugged. He didn't care what the officers did as long as they left him alone. They were only doing what they needed to stay alive, too. San Francisco was a tough town.

"I don't want you to murder nobody, but you got to be willin' to pull the trigger if it comes to that."

They walked along the street, heading back to the Embarcadero. Underwood seemed determined to go to a five-story brick building, edging Slocum back in that direction every time he tried to veer away. Rather than break openly with Underwood, he let the old sailor have his way. Since he had no job or prospects—he didn't even have a horse—he had nothing to lose by letting the man bend his ear awhile longer.

"Spit it out. What do you want from me?"

"I told you. I get a finder's fee if I bring 'im a man worth hirin'. Truth is, there are thousands of men in San Francisco willin' to kill for the price of a drink. Them's not the ones needed since they'll turn and run at the first sign of trouble."

"Are you recruiting for a filibuster? I don't want any part of that."

"What? No," Underwood said, laughing heartily. "You're the first who's ever thought that, but it makes sense. There's no intent on invadin' another country and takin' it over. Shows you're the sort needed, you comin' up with an idea like that, though. You don't rely on your fists or your gun alone. You think on matters. That's the kind of man Mr. Collingswood needs most, especially right now."

They came to a halt in front of the tall building. Emblazoned in gilt paint on the glass doors was the Central California Railroad logo, a bear blowing steam out its ears as it dragged along a passenger car.

"Your boss is looking to hire railroad bulls?"

"Better than that. You have experience out on your own. You ever work as a scout? I see by your expression you have. For the cavalry?"

"Once or twice. I also scouted for a government mapping expedition. Mostly, I've worked as a wrangler."

"Long days in the saddle, a keen eye for picking up a fugitive's trail, willing to use your six-shooter—you're exactly what Mr. Collingswood is in serious need of in a new employee."

They entered the lobby. A man behind a low desk looked up. He sneered at Slocum, but his expression changed when he saw Underwood.

"Afternoon, sir," he said. Slocum was sure he wasn't the one being addressed.

"Are they treatin' you good, Jason?"

"Not a bit of trouble, sir. You got another recruit? For the hunt?"

The way he spoke put Slocum on guard. He looked at Underwood, who raised his injured hand so his index finger pressed into his lips, cautioning the man to silence. A broad wink completed the act.

"Got it, Mr. Underwood."

"The boss man in his office?"

"He is, sir. Go right on up. And thank you. I do appreciate you gettin' me this here job. Without it, me and Mary Lou would be out on the street, starvin'."

Underwood made a vague salute that might have been nothing more than brushing a fly off his forehead, then moved so that Slocum had to dodge around him if he wanted to go back out into the street. No wrangler ever herded cattle with more skill. Ahead down a narrow corridor was a closed door with cantilever metal links that did nothing to muffle a coughing sound from the basement.

"You ever see one of these? An elevator. We don't have to go up the stairs. We can ride in style."

The gate opened and a uniformed man stepped back to let Slocum and Underwood inside. Slocum hesitated.

"Go on, John. It ain't a jail cell." This produced chuckles from both the uniformed man in the elevator cage and Underwood. "If anything, it's a new way of freedom. It's the future, or that's what Mr. Collingswood tells me."

Slocum stood with his feet wider than normal. When the cage lurched, he took the acceleration by bending his knees. He reached out and steadied himself as the car continued its upward clanking journey.

"Got a steam engine down in the cellar. Runs the goldangest series of wheels, gears, and pulleys you ever did see. Reckon they don't have things like this out when you're ridin' herd."

"I've heard of these. I never saw one before." Slocum tried to peer out and down into the cellar. Choking fumes rose in the shaft. Before he could clear his throat, the cage clattered to a halt and the uniformed operator pulled back the cantilever grate over the door.

"We're here. Come on. Mind your step, wipe your feet." Underwood chuckled again. "Just joshin' you on that. But Mr. Collingswood gets testy if you track onto his fancy rug."

Slocum took in the surroundings, wondering what it all cost. The rug was intricately threaded and looked like one he had heard called a Persian. Oil paintings on the walls showed people Slocum didn't recognize, but he liked some of the marble statues of naked women on low tables. Then he stopped at the far end of the hall where it opened out into a larger anteroom.

Naked women chiseled from cold white rock was one thing. The woman behind the desk talking quietly with Underwood was something else. She was vibrant, alive, and so lovely Slocum wanted to reach out and touch her flawless cheek, just to be sure she was real. Her eyes were bluer than the sky stretching over San Francisco Bay, and not a single raven-wing dark hair was out of place. Around her slender throat she wore a single strand of pearls, but this was only a ploy to slow the dive of his eyes to the deep valley between her breasts. Her scoop-necked blouse allowed the barest hint of the silky skin to plump up and outward. Or maybe the pearls ensured that anyone's gaze was properly directed to those well-formed breasts. Slocum had the feeling that nothing this woman did was by accident.

The papers on her desk were precisely stacked. Two books at the right side were carefully aligned. He saw one was a dictionary with a dozen small scraps of paper marking pages for future reference. Rather than looking up words a second time, she had found a way to reduce the time leafing through the book. The other title was hidden from him by the base of an unlit oil lamp. What caught his attention was a partly opened desk drawer. The glint of light off a blue gun barrel told him she was more than just an ornament decorating the outer office.

"This here is Mr. John Slocum, come to see Mr. Collingswood about a job." Underwood sounded pleased as punch when he made the introduction, as if the woman knew who Slocum was and would be impressed.

"For the great hunt?" The woman's musical voice enchanted Slocum as surely as her loveliness. She shifted slightly in her chair and pushed shut the drawer holding the pistol. That made it seem as if he had been accepted and was no longer a threat.

To her? Or to the man in the office?

But as bedazzled as he was by her beauty, he didn't miss how the job had gone from "the hunt" mentioned by the guard below to "the great hunt" referred to by the woman just outside the boss's inner sanctum.

"Underwood hasn't told me anything about this job. What's it all about?" He stepped back a half pace and read the nameplate on her desk. "Miss Crittenden."

"That's something Mr. Collingswood must discuss personally with you," she said. She gave him a quick scouting from where his boots crushed the expensive carpet up to his green eyes. "It's not up to me, sir, but if it were, you'd be hired immediately."

"Much obliged, Tamara, for your endorsement," Underwood said. "Can we go right in?"

She reached under her desk. Slocum heard a distant buzz like the signal on a telegrapher's key announcing an incoming message. He turned toward it. The buzz sounded inside Collingswood's office.

"That's a handy dingus," Slocum said. "Nobody sneaks up on him?"

"Not with me sitting here," Tamara Crittenden said. She looked over her shoulder, then back at Slocum. "Go right in, Mr. Slocum."

"You coming along?" Slocum asked Underwood.

"Do I look like anyone's fool? Why talk with the boss when I can stand out here and talk with the purtiest filly in town?"

This made Slocum laugh, joining in the other man's obvious enjoyment of the entire situation. Then he settled himself, took the crystal doorknob in his hand, twisted, and stepped into the room. For a moment, Slocum thought he had stepped into another world completely separate from the one of bustling Market Street, dead bodies, and crooked policemen.

The hallway from the elevator had been lined with expensive items. The rug under his feet had made him feel as if he walked on clouds. But here it was as much a change as stepping from the elevator. He resisted the urge to take off his boots and wiggle his bare toes in the rug's nap. Stepping on moss seemed uncouth by comparison. The two outer walls of the office were almost all plate glass window. One looked out over the Embarcadero and beyond, to San Francisco Bay with its freighters and tall-masted sailing ships in dock or waiting out in the middle of the Bay.

The other decorations had been kept to a minimum. Two

low tables held strange dwarf trees all bent up in a style Slocum had seen over in Japantown. The oak desk was polished so hard he had to squint against the reflection of the afternoon sun.

"You like the trees? Bonsai. That one is two hundred years old. The other is newer. Only fifty years old. Both were brought from Edo by a gardener I employed until he died."

"You took the trees then?"

"He willed them to me. That's the way it's done. These are heirlooms."

"You keep your possessions real close to you, don't you?" Slocum had heard talk like this before.

David Collingswood, or so read the nameplate on this desk, was dressed to the nines in an outfit Slocum knew wouldn't be out of place at the Union Club. In the midst of his impeccable jacket, vest, and ruffled shirt shone a headlight diamond bigger than any Slocum had ever seen worn by the most prosperous gambler. The difference was the gambler carried his wealth against the time his luck dried up. Collingswood wore this to hold his cravat in place. Slocum wondered if the man had a dozen more like it at home, maybe up on Russian Hill, where the richest of the rich in San Francisco lived.

A man like this was the sort to hire Tamara Crittenden to guard his doorway. And maybe there was more to their relationship beyond work. It made sense. Somehow, Slocum felt a bit disappointed in that notion.

"I have a reputation for selling dearly and buying cheaply," the man said. He sank into his leather chair and closed his eyes. For a moment he looked twenty years older than the forty that Slocum guessed. He opened his eyes and stared almost forlornly at Slocum. "You carry yourself well. You wouldn't have made it this far if you couldn't use that side arm well and perform the rest of the services I require."

"You trust Underwood that much?"

"With my life, if necessary. But his real ability comes in sizing up men."

"Like Miss Crittenden, too?"

Collingswood lifted an eyebrow, and a small smile danced on his lips. He perked up as he leaned forward, forearms on his desk. Before, he had just stared at Slocum—or through him. Now he gave him as thorough a once-over as Tamara Crittenden had.

"All the trappings of wealth mean nothing to you, do they?" Collingswood had finished his appraisal and sounded as if he were delivering a report to his board of directors.

"If I have food in my belly and a roof over my head, I'm happy."

"Not true, sir. The part about the roof. You prefer the open sky, the endless range, to roofs and walls. Underwood must have determined your tracking skills are what I need."

"What is this 'great hunt' you're hiring men for?"

"What makes you think there are more than just you?" Collingswood looked sharply at him. "What have you heard?"

"You're edgy about something. Underwood never said as much, but I got the sense that he had brought you other men for this hunt. You look like a belt and suspenders fellow. You don't take unnecessary risks."

"I got here by taking calculated risks, yes, but you are right about the job. And I take it as a personal affront when something is stolen from the railroad."

Slocum said nothing. He hadn't heard of a recent robbery. That meant Collingswood either quashed the story for the railroad to protect its—and his—reputation, or what had been stolen was more a matter of pride than value.

"The train was carrying a load of silver from Virginia City bound for a company bank vault here in San Francisco. The robbers got away with the entire shipment."

"You want me to track down the robbers? Or to get back the silver?"

"There are several others already hired to find the shipment and return it. While bringing the outlaws to justice is important, returning the shipment is paramount."

"How much silver was stolen?"

"Close to ten thousand dollars' worth."

Slocum simply stared at the railroad officer. Most men he knew could live pretty well on a few hundred dollars a year. This was an unimaginable fortune.

"How many robbers?" Slocum finally asked.

"The number is uncertain since those who would have been able to know are dead. The engineer guessed at four."

A welter of questions ran through Slocum's head, but he held them back.

"One hundred dollars a month, plus supplies and a reward if you return the shipment."

"How much would the silver weigh?"

"The point of the robbery was rocky and the road ran along a steep cliff. All I can believe is that they had freight wagons to move the silver."

"What's to keep me from finding the outlaws and keeping the silver?"

Collingswood glared at him, then said coldly, "Underwood found you. He can find ten more to track you down and kill you. However, you seem intelligent and are likely a man of your word. If you get the job, do you give your word to return the stolen silver?"

"I give value for my work," Slocum said. "Why haven't you sent out the law to find the robbers? A federal marshal could mount a posse for the money you're offering me."

"I have my reasons. Do you accept?"

"I do." Slocum shook hands with the railroad vice president and was surprised at both his strong grip and the calluses there. Underwood hadn't exaggerated. This was a man who sat atop a tall building looking over the harbor but had worked his way up there.

"Miss Crittenden will give you the details and an advance on your first month's pay."

"This won't take more than a month. I either find the robbers and the silver by then or I can't do it at all."

"Your honesty is refreshing, Mr. Slocum." David Collingswood turned in his chair to stare out the window through the Golden Gate. What he saw out on the Pacific, Slocum didn't know. It might have been anything or nothing as other matters consumed him.

Slocum took his leave, anticipating another talk with Tamara Crittenden. To his disappointment, both she and Underwood were gone. In the center of her desk was a large envelope with *John Slocum* written on it in a flowing feminine script.

He picked it up and saw a sheaf of papers, a map, and five ten-dollar gold pieces.

A clanking sound made him look down the corridor. The woman entered the elevator cage and disappeared down. Slocum hesitated, then wondered what sent her scurrying away from her post in the middle of the afternoon. He found the stairwell and raced down the steep steps as fast as he could go. He made it to the lobby in time to see Tamara leaving the building through the Market Street door.

Not bothering to examine his motives, Slocum ran after her.

3

Slocum stepped out into the street and looked in both directions, hunting for Tamara Crittenden. The woman's quick departure struck him as out of the ordinary. If David Collingswood wanted him to find the owlhoots responsible for stealing so much silver, he had to be aware of anything unusual.

He turned and caught sight of her rounding the corner farther toward the dock area. A woman as well dressed as she was asked for trouble going down there, even in the daytime. Slocum's long legs devoured the distance to the corner. He rounded it and skidded to a halt. Tamara spoke with a man not ten feet away. Her back was to Slocum. The man was roughly dressed and carried a six-shooter slung at his side. From the way he stood, the man was within an inch of drawing his gun in spite of no one nearby threatening him—or Tamara. This told Slocum the man's uneasiness came from being in San Francisco and not from anything immediate.

He understood that foreboding sensation. He felt it himself.

The man took Tamara by the arm. She pulled back, stood

her ground, and then went with him. Slocum followed a dozen paces behind, but he walked a trifle faster to narrow the gap so he could eavesdrop.

". . . specials," the dark-haired woman said. "You've got to get out of town."

"I don't care squat about specials. If Collingswood had any sense, he would have had an army on that train."

"You know why he didn't," Tamara said. The uneasiness in her voice caused Slocum to halt. She was more involved with something Collingswood knew nothing about than was healthy for her. All Slocum could figure was that this had to be one of the train robbers, and Tamara was involved up to her plucked, arched eyebrows.

"The others all lit out. It's just us," the man said.

"Please, Jack. I don't dare leave right now. He would be suspicious."

"You should never have got involved with him. Not like that."

"I didn't have any choice. We needed what he knew."

"That makes you into some kind of whore, Tam."

She spun on the man and slapped him hard. The sound echoed like a gunshot and drew attention all around. Slocum pressed himself against a building to keep from being seen as Jack looked about wildly. The expression on his face, the set to his shoulders, and the fierceness in his eyes said this wasn't a man who took such abuse. Slocum touched the ebony handle of his Colt Navy, ready to throw down if the man started to whale on the woman.

To Slocum's surprise, Jack's anger faded, and he touched his reddened cheek.

"I'm sorry. Shouldna said nuthin' like that to you. We all did what we had to."

"You killed those men. You told me there wouldn't be any shooting," Tamara said angrily.

"There wasn't any choice. A couple of them dyin' was pure bad luck on their part. But it's over. Come with me right now, Tam. We kin be across the Bay and headin' north 'fore Collingswood gets wind of it."

"He's got eyes everywhere. I do declare, Underwood is like Argus."

"I don't know what you mean. Let's leave now, and you can explain that to me. You got the book learnin'."

"You can learn, too, Jack. You're smart." She moved closer. Slocum missed much of what the woman said, but the way she pressed close against Jack took away any need for the exact words.

After a spell where Slocum heard nothing but seagulls squawking above, the slosh of the tide against the docks, and the heavy wagons in the street, Tamara's words came clear enough again for him to hear.

"Smart enough to take up with you," Jack said, but something in his words put Slocum on guard. "I'll wait until you give him notice."

"That might be a week, Jack."

"You do that, and we'll leave here. Together."

Tamara chanced a quick kiss, then cut across the street and melted in with the crowd. Slocum's senses came fully alert. He had heard double-crosses before, and Jack handed the woman one as sure as the sun shone down on San Francisco Bay.

He hesitated, looking after the woman. Catching her wouldn't be hard since she hadn't much of a head start on him, but the envelope with the pay for finding the train robbers and returning the stolen silver rested in his left hand. He looked up. Jack wasn't in any hurry to go anywhere. Slocum pulled out the map in the package and stuffed it into a coat pocket. The ten-dollar gold pieces slipped into a vest pocket. The rest was a contract he barely glanced at. He stuffed that into his other coat pocket as Jack finally turned and walked away.

The outlaw's gait changed from slow to determined. He had reached a conclusion. It had to be about leaving Tamara in the city on her own—possibly with David Collingswood.

The outlaw hadn't taken it well when he mentioned the railroad vice president and how Tamara wanted to stay to deflect suspicion. To Slocum, that said Tamara was playing another hand, one hidden from the outlaw.

And Jack realized it.

Slocum walked faster and closed the gap between them. He was so intent on getting to the man he failed to notice a scrawny rat-faced man move from a doorway into his path. Slocum collided with him, stumbled, and swung around to keep his balance. This put him into the arms of a burly sailor. The man smelled of the sea and dead fish and had arms like a sailing ship's anchor chain. They closed around him, pinning his arms to his side.

"Here, Knothole," said the rat man.

The sailor swung Slocum around off his feet and pressed his face into a rough brick wall.

"Hang on tight while I get his money. I seen him puttin' some coins in his vest pocket 'bout here."

A hand more like a boneless tentacle slipped between Slocum and the wall, searching for his vest pocket. The man worked as a pickpocket to be as deft as he was at plucking the coins from the pocket.

Slocum grunted, strained, and saw immediately how impossible it was to break free. He lifted one boot heel and raked his spur along the sailor's leg. The man cried out in pain. The next time Slocum kicked back, he drove the rowel into the man's flesh and felt hot blood begin to spurt. The pain forced the sailor to relax his grip the tiniest amount. Slocum got his other foot up, kicked hard against the wall, and sent them both stumbling away from the pickpocket.

Landing with his butt in the sailor's stomach knocked the wind from him. Slocum tried to stand and found his spur was entangled in the man's muscled calf. Not caring what damage he did, he kicked hard and pulled the spur free, rolled to his hands and knees, and came to a crouch.

The pickpocket had lifted the fifty dollars and wasn't

waiting around to help his partner. The last Slocum saw was the man's dark hair flying behind like a greasy banner as he raced away, skidding around a corner and disappearing.

"My leg. You ripped off my leg," the sailor moaned.

Slocum kicked the man in the ribs to give him something else to think about. Then he drew his Colt, cocked it, and aimed between the man's deep-set eyes.

"Your partner stole my money."

"I don't know Wellesley. I swear I don't!"

Slocum didn't bother arguing. The two worked as a team. He could shoot the sailor and nobody on the docks would pay much attention, but that let the rat-faced man get away scot-free.

"How much money you have on you? You and him been working hard today stealing other men's money?"

"I . . . All I got's this." The sailor fumbled out a few silver cartwheels. Slocum was alert for the man dropping them as a diversion. He kicked out and knocked the sailor flat onto the ground again. "Please, mister, I got a family. I—"

"Shut up." Slocum knelt and picked up four silver dollars. Then he patted down the sailor and got a gold double eagle. It wasn't near what he'd lost, but he wasn't totally broke because of the two street lurchers.

The sailor bled profusely onto the dirty street. The dust soaked up his life's blood like a sponge, leaving only dark lumps. Slocum lowered his six-shooter but held it at his side.

"The next time I see you or Wellesley, you'll be heavier by a couple ounces of lead in your thieving bellies." He kicked the sailor again, then stepped back.

The man scrambled to his feet the best he could. The injured leg dragging behind, he lumbered off venting curses learned over a long time at sea. Slocum saw how he rounded the same corner where his partner had gone. They likely had a hideout in that direction. When the sailor caught up with his cowardly partner, more blood would flow. Slocum only wished he could have gotten his fifty dollars back.

Still, he wasn't entirely down on his luck again. Going back to David Collingswood and asking for the balance of his month's pay wouldn't do, though Slocum wondered if Tamara had returned immediately to the office. She had met Jack to tell him about the railroad vice president hiring a small army to track down the robbers. That involved her in the robbery, but she was on her way to being cut out entirely because she had warned her partner.

Slocum shook his head. It amazed him how gullible women could be—and men. Collingswood had undoubtedly told Tamara all the details of the silver shipment. She had passed them along to Jack. The outlaw had a yen for her, but was it anything like the one she had for him? Slocum doubted that. When she had refused to come away with him, the outlaw's attitude had shifted. Wherever he went now, it was without Tamara.

Slocum walked fast, head swiveling around as he hunted for the outlaw. Losing him because of the two cutpurses rankled, but Slocum knew a few things that kept him looking. Jack wasn't a sailor, not from the way he dressed. His slightly bowed legs spoke of long days in the saddle, not hauling cable or furling sails on a ship. Wherever Tamara had met him was on land. He might have come into the Central California Railroad office. A railroad foreman? That might put him into contact with the woman.

How and where Jack and Tam had teamed up mattered little at the moment. The outlaw was deserting her. That meant he was hightailing it for wherever the silver had been stashed. Such a huge load required a couple freight wagons to move, if Collingswood's description was to be believed. If Slocum had to, he could ask around at towns along the tracks for a man matching Jack's description who had bought a heavy wagon and a team. High in the mountains meant that oxen might be a better choice than horses. They were slow but powerful, able to haul heavy loads up steep inclines.

All this flashed through Slocum's head as he walked along the docks. Jack had come this way for a reason other than to go in a direction opposite Tamara's when they parted.

"He's leaving San Francisco," Slocum said to himself. A slow grin curled his lips. The ferry across the Bay to Berkeley was an obvious way to flee.

It took him a few minutes to backtrack along the docks and find the Ferry Building. The next ferry left in a half hour. If Slocum found Jack before then, the outlaw would give up all the answers to the identity of his partners and where the silver had been hidden before the sun went down. He touched the knife sheathed at the small of his back. He knew ways of making a statue scream for mercy. He hadn't been a prisoner of the Apaches for damned near a week without learning some vicious tricks.

Slocum studied the crowd forming to buy tickets. At first he didn't see Jack and hung back. When he finally spotted the outlaw in line to buy a ticket, he knew what he had to do. Following the train robber to where he had stashed the silver was what he had been paid to do. If Jack led him to the rest of the gang, Slocum was in deep clover. David Collingswood hadn't given an exact amount for a reward, but bringing in the gang along with the stolen Virginia City shipment had to be significant. Collingswood was confident enough that Slocum wouldn't steal the silver himself.

There wasn't any reason to do that because Slocum knew he had a lever to use against the railroad officer. Collingswood hadn't let word of the robbery get out because his boss would hold him personally liable. That fit in even better with Collingswood engaging in a bit of pillow talk with Tamara. That made it seem as if the vice president was part of the robbery. Even if he weaseled out of any charges, he would be fired for being so stupid and thinking with his dick and not his head.

Slocum waited for Jack to get his ticket and shuffle toward the edge of the dock. The ferry wouldn't load for another twenty minutes, but the crowd was significant enough to hide him from sight. He slid a silver dollar across and got back two bits with his ticket, then went to find a spot where he could spy on Jack without being noticed.

He found it by a pillar holding up the northern side of the dock. The ferry was a huge two-story side-wheel steamboat rivaling anything he had seen on the Mississippi. Slocum settled down, hat pulled low on his forehead so he could look around without exposing his face. Jack hadn't seen him, but if he intended following him to the ends of the earth, being recognized later as the man from the ferry taking too much interest in the outlaw would only cause trouble.

The ferry let out a gout of steam, and the whistle began its high-pitched shrieking. The crewmen lowered chains on a loading platform and let the crowd surge onto the broad decks. Slocum waited for Jack to disappear inside the cabin, where benches lined the walls and a bar at the far end served beer and whiskey, before going to board himself. He stopped dead in his tracks and stared. He pulled his hat lower and turned away so he cast a sidelong look as Tamara Crittenden boarded the ferry.

Only when she had passed over her ticket did Slocum board, but he wondered at the way she looked about furtively, as if seeking out Jack—and wanting to avoid him. She had changed into riding clothes. From the weight of her purse, she carried the pistol that had been in her desk drawer.

When Jack appeared on the top deck and leaned on the railing, Tamara quickly lowered her head and ducked behind a large man in a threadbare suit, using him as a shield.

Slocum wondered at the game of cat and mouse being played out. Tamara didn't want Jack spotting her. And Slocum followed both the woman and her outlaw lover. The ferry lurched, forcing him to grab on to a railing. This was getting more interesting by the minute.

4

Slocum hunched over and tried not to stand out in the crowd. Being six feet tall put him half a head above most men. Seeing his battered Stetson bobbing along might draw unwanted attention from Jack or, more worrisome for Slocum, Tamara Crittenden. She was the wild card in a hand he played in a game without knowing the rules. She had obviously played a role in the silver robbery, but was she now acting as a spy for David Collingswood? Why did she cozy up to Jack, then secretly follow him? Slocum considered the possibility that Collingswood had an entire posse of men out hunting for the train robbers and still used his secretary for the same goal without letting anyone else know.

The questions made Slocum's curiosity bump itch something fierce. He had lost some money to the street thieves, but even if he had been flat broke, he would have pressed on to find the answers to questions bubbling up in his head. That Tamara was a lovely woman didn't hurt, but she had no problem stealing from her employer. That made her as dangerous as Jack and the rest of his gang.

The crowd pushed across the deck and onto the pier.

Slocum let the people carry him along. He exited before the two he trailed, so he eased away from the crush and found a spot down the street where he could watch carefully for Jack and Tamara. He had to wait only a few seconds for Jack. The outlaw rushed away, head down and intent on some unknown destination. Slocum let out a sigh of relief. The man had been only a few yards behind on the boat. But Slocum held his position until Tamara stepped onto dry land. She had eyes only for Jack as he coursed down the street. She passed within a few yards, never noticing Slocum.

He started after her, then realized how much of a disadvantage he would be at if Jack went to a livery and mounted up. He considered stealing a horse, but that would cause such a ruckus, even Tamara, intent on her robber boyfriend, would notice. He edged down the side of the street opposite Tamara. If he kept her in sight, following Jack would take care of itself.

When the woman broke into a run, he knew what had happened. Jack had reclaimed his horse and was on his way out of town. Oakland was a busy town, the terminus of the ferry from San Francisco and depot to a half-dozen railroad lines.

Slocum fumbled in his coat pocket and pulled out one of the papers that he'd been given. He scanned the bottom sheet signed by David Collingswood and changed directions, going to the Central California Railroad Station. He found it amid a tangle of tracks from other lines, but the station house was well marked and prosperous-looking with a long line of passengers waiting to buy tickets for a train heading over the mountains and going eastward in the direction of Virginia City along the main line.

Slocum took the steps three at a time and pushed through the side door. The stationmaster glared at him for the disturbance.

"You get on out of here," the man said. He barely topped five feet, was rotund, and had walrus mustaches that twitched to show his choler at Slocum's invasion of his sanctuary.

"I need a horse," Slocum said.

"You been out in the sun too long, mister? This is a railroad station. We got iron horses. Puff, puff, choo, choo? You wait in line out on the platform and buy a ticket like everybody else." The stationmaster thrust out a stubby finger to show Slocum where to go.

Slocum pulled out the page and held it up for the man to read. The stationmaster moved his eyeglasses down on his nose, reared back, and read.

"Son of a bitch," he said. "I ain't seen one of those in a month of Sundays."

"It's authorization for me to commandeer whatever I need. I want a horse and tack."

"Suppose there must be one around back."

"Show me."

The stationmaster bristled at the sharp order, but Slocum had been a captain in the CSA and had learned command in more dire situations. The man glanced from the letter to Slocum's grim visage and decided that determination meant more than anything a vice president of the railroad might write. He grunted as he pushed himself to his feet, then went to a back door. He threw it open and shoved his stubby finger out.

"That one. Take that one, and be damned sure I am going to bill the home office for it."

"Make it to Miss Tamara Crittenden's attention. She handles all of Mr. Collingswood's money problems."

Slocum spent a few minutes getting to know the horse, letting it know it had a new rider. He adjusted the stirrups and then stepped up. The saddlebags were filled with odd tools. The horse's previous rider—owner?—had worked as a repairman. What little food had been stuffed into the saddlebags wouldn't last a day out on the trail.

That was a problem to be taken care of later. He

discarded the tools and scooped up a rifle leaning against a shed, perhaps left there by a railroad guard. Outfitted as well as he was likely to be, Slocum put his heels to the horse's flanks and got it trotting from the railroad station. He returned to the main street leading from the docks and rode along until he saw a livery stable. He called out to a stableboy struggling to move a bale of hay.

"You put up a horse for a man wearing a six-shooter?" He went on and described Jack the best he could.

"Yeah, he left his horse here yesterday. Said he wasn't gonna be back for a week, but he just now picked it up and rode off. Him and Mr. Wright got into a tussle over how much to pay." The boy chuckled. "Mr. Wright got him to fork over half a week's boarding fee. From what I could tell, he paid in silver." The boy scratched his head, then wiped away perspiration. "Not a nugget neither. This was like he had shaved off a slice or two from a solid bar. I've seen coins and I've seen scrapings from a silver vein, but this wasn't nothin' like that."

"Which direction did he go? Did he say?"

"Was headin' o'er the hills, goin' to Sacramento, he said. Well, I overheard him say that. Don't tell Mr. Wright I was spyin'!"

"What about the woman who came right on his heels?"

A dreamy expression came to the boy's face. Tamara had been here. Words weren't needed to confirm that.

"Did she buy a horse?"

"Yeah, she did. Mr. Wright wanted to dicker."

"So he could keep her here a bit longer," Slocum guessed.

"He ain't nobody's fool. 'Course he wanted her to stick around a spell. She was quite a looker. But she paid him the first price he asked. That made him mad."

Slocum had to laugh. Horse trading often went on all day long, both sides enjoying the ebb and flow of arguments and observations about the quality of the horseflesh being purchased and even the legitimacy of both buyer and seller's heritage. Tamara had been in a rush to get after Jack and had paid the asking price. Slocum guessed she wasn't used to such haggling either, at least not with money. Her price came higher, much higher, and had little to do with greenbacks.

Unless he was completely mistaken, she had worked her way into Collingswood's office to get the time and schedule for the silver shipment. Whether she knew a big shipment was due or had worked her way up the corporate ladder and simply waited for a decent opportunity hardly mattered. The more he thought on it, the more he thought she had told Jack and his gang about the shipment, and they had double-crossed her. Now she wanted her share—or all of it.

He found a single road leading due east through the hills and took it, keeping the horse trotting along. The mare had no trouble with him astride, making him believe the repairman might have been heavier. Getting rid of most of the tools in the saddlebags had lightened the load, too. He only wished there had been time to lay in provisions for what might turn into a long pursuit.

It only took an hour for him to spot the woman riding along a mile ahead on the mountainous road. He caught sight of her as she took a sharp bend some distance above him. The way she rode, she paid no attention to her back trail. Jack had to be ahead of her because Slocum saw no trace of the man trailing her. He began the climb up the side of the hill, losing track of Tamara, but unlike her, he kept a close watch on his back trail. The way Collingswood had hired other railroad detectives meant Slocum had company. He just didn't know who they might be—and they had no idea who he was. When such a haul was at stake, shooting first and asking questions later was the easier trail to ride.

Slocum thought hard as he trotted along the switchback road. The vice president had to be desperate to hire men recruited by Underwood, unless he trusted the two-fingered man more than he would a simple employee. Underwood might be a good judge of character but how many men were like Slocum, who would find such a trove and return it for a small reward?

He was a man of honor, and he had promised to find the silver for the railroad.

He came out on the crest of the hill and was treated to a fine view of the eastern slopes. The road went down steeply, almost straight as an arrow. Tamara rode with the same resolve the sheriff had shown before. Squinting, Slocum made out another solitary rider much farther along the road. It took little imagination to believe this was Jack. Since he rode alone, he would be easy prey. Even with a gang backing him up, Slocum thought it would be easy to get the drop on him.

Night crept up on him, but Slocum pressed on because both Tamara and Jack did also. He tried to keep from falling asleep in the saddle, but a bigger problem was his horse. As game as the mare was to keep going, it started to stumble, as much from exhaustion as the dark.

Slocum gave in to the inevitable. Either he stopped for the night to rest the mare or he walked when the horse died under him. He found a narrow game trail that crossed the road, and he followed it for a quarter mile. His approach scared away smaller animals. A cougar snarled and stared at him. The last light of day caught the cat's eyes and turned them bright silver. Slocum touched his six-shooter but knew the odds of killing the cougar were slim if it attacked. A gust of breath escaped his lungs when the cat slunk off, still snarling.

He let his horse drink while he kept careful watch. Farther upstream darted furtive creatures. Slocum made sure his horse's reins were secured to a limb before picking up a rock and quietly stalking a fat rabbit. A quick strike and he ate well that night.

Not knowing where Tamara had gone in her hunt for the train robber made him wary of keeping more than a low fire going that night. However, the breeze coming off the higher slopes was cold enough to make him throw caution to the wind. He built a large enough fire to keep him and the mare warm through the night.

With his blanket pulled around his shoulders, he slipped away into deep sleep, dreaming of silver . . . and Tamara Crittenden.

He came awake with a start, cursing himself because the sun had been up for an hour. The horse had eaten its fill of grass growing along the stream bank. Slocum's belly grumbled, but the need to catch up with the woman drove him past such minor discomfort. He saddled the mare, stepped up, and trotted down the road, wondering how far back he had fallen. With every crossing road he stood to choose the wrong direction and end up searching aimlessly.

Then he heard a steam whistle in the distance, drew rein, and slowly turned to locate the tracks. The train had to run less than a mile off to his right. The robbery had taken place miles farther east. If the gang hid the silver, it would be closer to the spot where they had stopped the locomotive. Jack had lit out of San Francisco, leaving Tamara behind. To Slocum that meant the robber wanted to grab the loot and hightail it away.

But why had he bothered going to San Francisco at all if he intended to double-cross her?

Too many questions and not a one of them had to be answered. Slocum intended to retrieve the stolen silver, capture or kill the robbers, then head back to San Francisco to collect his reward. He patted the mare's neck and headed up into another ridge of hills. These might be considered mountains. Underwood had said the Celestials working on the Central California Railroad had dangled from baskets as they chipped away the sides of the hills to create a railroad bed where none had been possible beforehand. From the sheer peaks and the steep slope that made his horse slow and eventually forced him to get off and walk a spell, he believed that. Cutting a road was one thing. A railroad required solid ground and no slope steeper than three or four percent—every hundred feet of run had less than four of rise. The locomotives were powerful, but not big enough to drag a long line of freight cars up anything steeper.

He reached the middle of the pass after noon, took a rest, then saw smoke rising from a cook fire not a hundred yards away. Hidden by the trees, whoever stoked the fire and boiled coffee presented Slocum with a dilemma. If this was another traveler, coming from the east, he could beg for a cup of that coffee and likely get it. However, he knew it was just as likely to be Tamara as a stranger.

Slocum tethered his horse, then followed his nose through the woods to a spot where he could push some thick underbrush away to see who rested in the clearing. He caught his breath. Jack poked at the fire, not a care in the world. The man had draped his six-shooter over a stump, along with his freshly washed shirt drying in the bright sunlight. This was the best chance Slocum would ever have of capturing him. Jack could never reach his six-gun in time to get off a shot if Slocum simply walked up on him.

But Jack had a gang still roaming around the hills. They had to know the railroad wouldn't let them remain free and that a posse hunted them. Slocum wondered how many men Collingswood had hired. From the sound of it, Slocum was in danger of rubbing elbows with a goodly number of hired gunmen.

Something else held him back. Unless Tamara had taken a wrong turn, he should have come on her before finding Jack. As resolute as she had been, Tamara had to be nearby. Losing Jack on the road would have been the last thing possible for her.

Slocum settled down, keeping a sharp eye out. Jack stretched, then went for his six-shooter but didn't put it on. Instead, he fumbled about and pulled a sheet of paper from a hidden pouch in the broad leather gun belt. Jack held it up and let the sun shine through the paper. Being too far away to see what was on the paper made Slocum edgy. After a few minutes, Jack replaced the sheet and stretched out on his blanket in the warm afternoon sun.

The soft rustle of movement through the undergrowth brought Slocum completely alert. His hand rested on his six-shooter. Tense, he watched as Tamara slipped into the clearing not ten feet from him. Again her concentration on the outlaw had saved him from being discovered. He waited to see what she did next.

Like a floating ghost, Tamara went to the stump. She patted the damp shirt, then moved on to the gun belt. It took all her willpower not to cry out when she found the hidden pouch and pulled out the sheet of paper. Like the outlaw, she held it up to the sun and then quickly tucked it where Slocum would gladly hunt to retrieve it. She settled her blouse, backed away, turned, and vanished into the woods.

Jack slept on the entire time he was being robbed.

Slocum considered his options. Capturing Jack would be a snap. Tamara had robbed him of what must be a map showing where the silver had been stashed. Getting the outlaw back to San Francisco and justice was one choice, but Slocum discarded it. Proving that Jack had any part in the train robbery would be his word against the outlaw's. He *knew* Jack was a thief but had no proof.

If he sat on the silver and waited for the outlaw to come get it, that would be the proof needed for a jury to convict. Slocum backed away into the forest, and within minutes was on the road going after Tamara.

Again he had to rely on common sense to figure which direction she took. Returning to San Francisco made no sense. She must have pressed on, riding eastward. Or she would cut over to the railroad. From what Slocum saw of the terrain, that route carried serious danger with it. The tracks had been laid on a shelf chipped from the side of a mountain, and riding alongside them added the danger of an approaching train. There was nowhere to get off the tracks to let the train pass safely.

He rode faster and caught sight of her as she left the main road. The double-rutted, weed-overgrown road she took must have been used by the railroad construction crew. His heart beat a little faster. Finding the silver cache was a matter of letting Tamara use the map, then swooping down on her. Slocum needed a better idea of what to do then, but much depended on how long it took her to find the stolen shipment.

As Slocum turned to follow, a cold knot formed in his gut. An instant later a shot rang out. Slocum's mare reared and threw him to the ground. He lay still in the weeds and dust.

5

Hoofbeats came closer. Slocum lay still, his mare trotting away. When a shadow passed over him, Slocum moved fast. Rolling, he came to his knees and drew his Colt Navy. He pointed it up at Jack and fired. The same fate came to Jack that had visited itself on Slocum. His shot missed but caused the horse to rear and throw the train robber to the ground.

Slocum tried to get a second shot off but had to dodge flying hooves as the outlaw's horse pawed at the air. By the time Slocum got to his feet and moved around the spooked horse, Jack had lit out across the road. Squaring off, Slocum lifted his six-shooter and fired. The bullet missed. Jack dodged at the last possible instant and dived for a gully. Knowing he couldn't keep up a protracted gunfight, Slocum ran after the robber, his gun ready for what had to be a killing shot. He was down to four rounds.

Jack poked up and Slocum shot. The outlaw's hat went flying, only to snap down when the chin string caught under Jack's nose. This threw off any return fire. Then Slocum dug in his toes and launched himself in a low dive. He hit the ground, skidded, and found his arms circling the man's shoulders. With a huge twist, he rolled Jack over and sent his six-gun flying.

"Give it up, Jack," Slocum grated out, hanging on for dear life. He couldn't bring his gun to bear and releasing his grip would prolong the fight. "I got you fair and square."

"Who the hell are you?"

"Sent by the Central California Railroad."

This caused a new surge of effort that flung Slocum around like a fish on a hook.

"I know Tamara," Slocum said in desperation as his grip slipped.

"What?"

This gave him the chance to get his balance back. With a heave, he upended Jack and threw him hard to the ground. The whoosh of air leaving the outlaw's lungs took some of the fight from him. Slocum got to his feet, then dropped one knee into the man's gut. Jack turned green and started to upchuck.

"Don't," Slocum said, shoving his Colt's muzzle into the man's face.

"Ga-ga-give up. I give up! Don't shoot."

Slocum backed away, the front sight centered between Jack's eyes. He found himself tossed on the horns of a dilemma. It was the same one he had faced before, back in San Francisco. He had followed the outlaw rather than Tamara, only to find she trailed Jack. But where did Slocum's duty lie? He had one of the train robbers in custody, but he couldn't prove it. He suspected Collingswood would never let Jack stand trial but would torture the silver's hiding place from him. Although he wouldn't do it himself, Underwood looked more than capable of carrying out the railroad vice president's orders using a flensing knife. Jack would be better served to make a deal and give up the silver in return for his freedom.

Slocum couldn't do that either. It had to be both the outlaw and the stolen silver shipment. He had taken the job from Collingswood with those as the reasons he was being paid.

"You robbed the train," Slocum said.

"I ain't sayin' a word. You can't prove it!"

"What's the map to you hid in your gun belt?"

Slocum laughed without humor at the expression on the man's face. He shoved his pistol forward to keep Jack from reaching under the broad leather belt for the map—which wasn't there.

"How'd you know about that?"

"Why'd you make a map when you know where you hid the silver?"

"I was gonna give Tamara her share, but she wanted more."

"Why?"

"I promised her fifty dollars and was going to give it to her, but she wanted a full share. None of us knew how much'd be in that shipment."

"She wanted half your share?" Slocum began to see how the double-crossing had come about. If anything, Jack was honest in paying off the source of his information. It had been Tamara who wanted more.

"Hell, no. She wanted a full share. One-fifth." Jack swallowed hard and paled when he realized how much he was confessing to. Now Slocum knew only four robbers had stopped the train. "I couldn't give her that much. We split it up, each of us taking a quarter."

"Where are the other three in your gang?"

"We lit out to every point of the compass. I don't know where they went, and now I'm damned sorry I went back to San Francisco."

Slocum felt a small pang of remorse for Jack. He could have hightailed it with the loot after the robbery but had been honest enough to offer Tamara her payment. The men robbing the train took the chance that there wouldn't be any—or not much—in the shipment. That they had hit the mother lode didn't diminish the risk they had taken of getting their heads blown off.

Then again, Jack's interest might have been more in Tamara than giving her what had been promised.

"How'd you and her cross trails?"

"You said you knew her. Figure it out. You're probably the next one in the chain of men she's used." Jack ran his finger under his belt and stopped about where the hidden pouch lay empty.

"She took the map," Slocum said. "I saw her."

Jack made a wild grab and confirmed what Slocum had told him.

"That bitch. I shoulda wrung her neck like a chicken destined for the stew pot. She refused to take the money I offered her. I never thought she would cheat me out of my entire share!"

The outlaw looked up at Slocum, then turned wary. He continued to finger the empty pouch sewn inside the gun belt.

"How'd you know she took it?"

"I saw her. She followed you from San Francisco. She must have known you were cutting her out of her share."

"She wanted it all! Greedy bitch."

Slocum's attention wavered for a split second. This was all it took for Jack to grab a dirt clod and fling it at him. The sod exploded in Slocum's face, forcing him to involuntarily turn away. Then he was bowled over as the robber tackled him around the knees. He landed as hard on the ground as Jack had. The fall momentarily stunned him. Then he gasped and fought to keep the grip on his wrist from turning his own weapon against him.

Jack sat astraddle Slocum's waist and used his weight to force the gun hand around. Slocum pulled the trigger and sent a round sailing past the man's ear. As his attention had flagged for an instant, now it was Jack's turn to react. He jerked away and gave Slocum all the opening he was likely to get. He arched his back and heaved. Somehow he fired again. This time the slug ripped into Jack's side. The man cried out in pain and sagged back.

Slocum kicked free and came to his knees, pistol aimed at the man. There was no need. Jack had gone white. He pressed his hand into his left side, but the flood of red spurting out between his fingers showed that Slocum had struck something important near the man's heart.

"You got me," Jack said in a weak voice. "I feel all wet inside." He coughed and then fixed a hard look on Slocum. "You kilt me. Grant a dyin' man's last request. Go kill her, too."

Slocum had no chance to respond. The outlaw slumped back, dead. This solved part of his dilemma about how to proceed. No honest jury would have convicted him of the robbery without more proof than Slocum's word. While he doubted Collingswood would allow an unbiased jury to hear the case—he would have wanted the silver shipment back more than seeing a robber thrown into San Quentin—taking Jack in would have given Slocum some satisfaction of a job getting done.

He sighed, took time to reload his six-shooter, then hunted around for a good place to bury the outlaw. He didn't even know the man's name other than what he had overheard when Tamara spoke with him near the Embarcadero. The better part of an hour saw Jack buried deep enough to keep the casual coyote or wolf from digging up the body. A rude cross marked the spot. Slocum didn't bother marking what little he knew of the outlaw on it. He was dead and that was enough for anyone passing by to know.

Not that any pilgrim on the road would even slow to wonder who had been buried anonymously.

Slocum found Jack's horse and rummaged through the saddlebags. The man had prepared better for the trail than Slocum had. After transferring the food to his own saddlebags, Slocum saw that what remained was worth keeping for himself, too. The hunks of silver had been hacked off an ingot. Without weighing it, Slocum guessed the silver was worth about fifty dollars. In that, Jack had been an honest thief. He had brought Tamara's due, only she had gotten greedy.

With the outlaw's map in her possession, she stood to get a lot richer. Slocum wished Jack had lived long enough to point him in the right direction, but common sense sent him riding along the trail toward the railroad tracks. If he found where Jack and his gang had driven away with the shipment, finding Tamara wouldn't be too hard. The silver had to be stashed somewhere nearby.

At least Jack's share had to be. The other three could have driven off in their wagons with their shares, but Jack had seen fit to take Tamara's cut. That meant the map the woman had taken led to a treasure cache.

As he rode, Slocum found himself with a new dilemma. Before, it had been finding the silver or taking Jack back to the railroad vice president without real proof of guilt. Now he might catch Tamara, but without the silver, it mattered nothing. He was certain she had supplied the robbers everything they needed to know to successfully rob the train, but the man who could have testified against her was buried under a few feet of California sod.

Trying to figure out whether he should worry more about returning the silver or taking the woman back to her boss occupied him as he rode. The railroad tracks appeared quicker than he thought. Then he realized how he had been drifting as he wrestled with a problem that might never exist. The tracks went up into a pass a couple miles off. Slocum took out a map from the envelope Collingswood had given him and tried to make out where the robbery had occurred.

He turned uphill and began riding, aware that he had little room on either side of the tracks to wait for any train coming through to pass. Now and then he dismounted and pressed his hand against the tracks to check for vibrations.

When he was a half mile from the summit, he came to the decision to press on and get past the narrow gap. He wished he'd had the foresight to get a railroad schedule when he had commandeered the horse back at the depot. No Central California Railroad coming through since he had ridden onto the tracks worried him.

He put his heels to the mare's flanks to get the sturdy horse moving faster. Jack's horse, tied to his saddle, balked. Slocum took a few minutes to tug on the other horse's reins to get it moving into the steep-walled pass. The horse kept trying to rear.

"What's wrong with you?" He dismounted and went to calm the horse. As he stepped on the tracks, he felt the quivers. The horse had already detected the oncoming train.

Slocum looked back down the slope he had scaled and didn't see an approaching train. That meant it was struggling up the eastern slope, coming into the narrow pass. The grade was considerable on the far side. Slocum knew that from hearing of the robbery. Jack and his gang had used that steep slope slowing the locomotive to climb aboard.

He had a quick decision to make. If he reached the far side of the pass, he had no way of knowing where he could get off the tracks to let the train pass. He looked back down the grade he had taken on the western side. He had a half mile to go to get to a widening where he could get free of the tracks.

Go on and pray for a spot to ride off the rails? Or go back down the way he had come?

Slocum was a gambling man, but his chances were better retreating. He swung into the saddle and turned the mare around. The rocky walls hadn't bothered him before. Now it felt as if he had been thrust into a stone grave.

A quarter mile of trotting got him out of the pass but still no space on either side of the tracks. Jack's horse tried to race past. He glanced behind and saw why. The locomotive crested the grade and sent plumes of billowing white smoke up from its stack. Slocum heard the change in the clangs and bangs from the engine. It had been straining before it hit the pass. Now it let out a relieved whistle and gathered speed on the downside—directly behind Slocum.

He bent low and got as much speed from his horse as he could. The tracks hummed as the locomotive gathered speed, having nothing but downgrade in front of it. Slocum winced as the engineer spotted him and began using his whistle to warn him away. Slocum urged his horse to greater speed. A quarter mile ahead lay a cleared area where workers must have camped. The mare strained now, lather flecking her heaving flanks. The engineer never tried to apply the brakes. It would take a mile to stop—and Slocum would be long dead by then. His only hope was the clearing.

"Come on," he shouted in the horse's ear as he bent over. "We can make it."

He charged for the clearing. And then Jack's horse let out a horrendous shriek that was almost human in its agony. The horse cartwheeled through the air past him. The cowcatcher on the front of the locomotive had served its purpose of clearing away anything that might otherwise be knocked down and pulled under the engine, fouling its wheels or derailing it.

Slocum rode faster. He felt the heat from the steam engine, cringed at the repeated whistle blasts, and rode for his life. The clearing was only a few yards ahead. A few. So close.

Hot cinders spewed from the smokestack and burned at his neck. He was a goner, run over as the horse had been.

6

Slocum screamed, but the cry disappeared in the whine of the steam engine rushing past. He fell from horseback, and the mare galloped on. For a moment, Slocum lay stunned, then realized he hadn't been run over by the train. The clatter of its steel wheels already receded down the tracks as it raced on toward the Oakland depot. He flopped back and stared upward, watching billowy white clouds string out into feathery strands and then vanish, leaving behind only sky. Pure blue. Clear. Sky.

He was still alive.

Forcing himself to sit up, he held out his hands. They were steady enough. He'd had more than one close shave in his day, but this one had come closer than most. Bits of Jack's horse were strewn about where the train had struck it and severed its front legs. A frantic neighing drew his attention to the back of the clearing. Trees boxed in his mare. He heaved to his feet and spent the next half hour calming the horse from its narrow escape with death. By the time he mounted and headed back up the slope, he was once more determined to find Tamara and the silver and take them both back to San Francisco. When he reached the pass again, he dropped off his horse to check for vibrations in the rail. Only warm steel stretched under his fingers.

He led his horse through the pass and looked down the western stretch of track. He understood why the train robbers had chosen this section. Even riding down was something of a chore, but he kept the horse moving. The mare shied once or twice, forcing Slocum to look over the brink and down into the deep canyon on one side of the track. The other side presented some difficulty in riding because of the thick undergrowth and steep stone wall rising more than twenty feet above his head.

When he reached the spot where Jack had to have robbed the train, he found ample evidence of how the gang had waited in a clearing and where the tracks were newly repaired from being twisted around by a car that had run away out of control. He reenacted the robbery—where the gang had attacked, how the last two cars had been unhooked, the way those cars had rolled backward down the incline.

Slocum tried to figure out where the mail clerk had gone. The only possible direction he could have gone, unless he was one of the gang, was down into the canyon. No one survived a fall like that. He fumbled out the report and read through it again. No mention was made of recovering the body for burial. All he saw were detailed reports on repairing the track and how the next two trains from Virginia City had been delayed.

He doubted either of them carried as much silver as the shipment already spirited away. That much silver represented weeks of mining output.

Riding downhill, he finally came to a more level section of tracks. He grinned crookedly when he saw a small firepit with embers still smoldering alongside the tracks. While this might have been left by others Collingswood had sent out, he doubted it. All he saw were the tracks of a solitary horse. When he dismounted and examined the soft earth more closely, he knew he had found Tamara's trail. The small footprint belonged to a woman, not some big galoot out hunting for train robbers.

Spiraling out from the campfire convinced him that Tamara had stopped for a quick meal and to rest her horse, then had ridden westward along the tracks. He picked up the pace, sure that she hadn't veered away. The tracks were still through mountainous terrain, and opportunities for going north or south were nonexistent because of the deep canyon and the rocky walls on either side. But a few miles west, Slocum saw that he had to do some clever tracking. A road crossed the tracks and went down each of the branching canyons.

Tamara hadn't done anything to hide her tracks. Slocum took the road north. The sunbaked dirt hid any hoofprints but he had a good feeling this was the way she had gone—it was the way she read off Jack's map. An hour along the road, he heard the burbling of a creek and knew he had to water his horse. He gave the mare its head and walked alongside. As the horse drank noisily, he splashed water on his face to get off dirt and cinders. Removing the stench of burned steel from his clothing had to wait until later when he could give both shirt and pants a good scrubbing.

As he started to pull the horse away, he heard a muffled curse. His hand went to his six-shooter, then he relaxed. Staking the horse by a patch of grass, he made his way through the woods. Only a few yards off the road he found Tamara. The woman had the map pinned to the ground with four rocks and looked from it up to distant peaks and then back at the map.

He watched her for a spell, drinking in her sleek figure and the way she bent over now and again to study the map. She finally moved the map around and turned in a different direction. When she stood facing away from him, her hands on her hips and still cursing up a blue streak, he crept up behind her.

"Lose something, Miss Crittenden?"

He laughed when she jumped a foot. She half turned and caught sight of him. With a surprisingly quick move, she thrust her hand into a coat pocket. Slocum was faster. He caught her wrist and held it motionless.

"Better not come out with a gun," he warned.

She relaxed, and he let her take her hand away. He stepped close and thrust his hand into her pocket. Pressed close, he felt her heart hammering as her breast crushed into his chest. Slocum might have fumbled around a bit more than necessary as he searched for her gun and then pulled it free. The movement of her hip through the fabric excited him, as did the nearness of his face to hers.

Tamara glared at him, put her hand on his chest, and pushed him away.

"Why did you frighten me like that?"

"I didn't want to end up with a bullet from this in my gut." He held up the small pistol, a Colt New Line loaded with seven .22-caliber bullets. Up close it could be deadly.

"I'd never do that," she said. "I'd aim between your eyes."

He laughed again. Honesty appealed to him. He tucked away her gun in his coat pocket and looked down at the map.

"I saw you steal that from Jack."

"Jackson? You're in it with him?" Tamara clamped her mouth shut and ground her teeth.

Slocum shook his head.

"You killed him? Jack's dead?"

"He resisted my attempt to take him back to Mr. Collingswood and the law for a proper trial."

"I wondered why he hadn't caught up with me. He knows where the silver is stashed, after all. Rather, he knew." Her despondency boiled out like heat from a fire.

"You and him?"

For a moment Tamara stared at him with her mouth open. She finally closed it to keep from catching flies. A sly look danced in her blue eyes.

"You don't miss much, do you? Did you see us in San Francisco?"

"You're quick on the uptake. That's how I got on your trail. I was on the same ferry across the Bay."

"Getting a horse couldn't have been easy, not with only fifty dollars in your pocket." She grinned. "I know what was in the envelope Mr. Collingswood left on my desk for you."

Slocum didn't bother telling her he was robbed before he got on the ferry. He had done well enough since, though the close call getting run over by the locomotive put that in question.

"Where's the silver?"

"Jack told me they split it up, the four of them. Each took as much as he could load onto his horse."

"No wagons?" Slocum frowned. "Did they bring pack mules?"

"I . . . I didn't know how big the shipment was. Jack and his gang weren't ready for so much. It turned into an embarrassment of riches. Nobody expected so much silver."

"So you're saying they all hid the silver instead of freighting it off? That's what the map's for?"

"I can't make head nor tail of it. Jack never said it was a map to where he hid his silver or even if it showed where the others had gone with theirs. But why would he make the map if he didn't want to remember where he'd put his share?" Tamara furrowed her brows as she concentrated on this conundrum.

"Why make a map at all? Did he intend to give it to you so you could find it?" Slocum read the answer on her face. Jackson had complained about how she wanted more than he was willing to share. He had no intention of giving a single ounce more to Tamara than they had agreed on before the robbery.

"Jack could get lost if he turned around. He had a terrible sense of direction. He must have hidden the silver and made the map to remind himself where it was."

Slocum had come across men who confused left and right. It still didn't set right with him that a man bold enough to make off with such a hoard of silver needed a map.

"You can't figure out what he did on the map?"

Tamara moved to keep him from picking up the map, but Slocum pushed her away. He looked at the map and saw how she had aligned it with the tallest mountain peaks surrounding them. The single line with bars through it had to be a crude depiction of the railroad tracks. Slocum stared off into the distance, checked the map, and looked back.

"If this is right, he hid the silver a couple miles in that direction."

"What are you going to do, John?" Tamara stood with her arms tightly crossed over her chest.

"My job. I was hired to catch the robbers and return the silver."

"Does that include me?"

"Mount up," Slocum said, folding the map and tucking it into his coat pocket. "We're going to fetch some silver stolen from the Central California Railroad."

He watched her closely, but she made no effort to run. When he was mounted, Slocum motioned for her to ride ahead. She hesitated, then obeyed.

"So," she called over her shoulder, "how do you intend to take the silver back to San Francisco? You have the same problem Jack did. Even if this is only his share, it'll be too heavy for us."

"I'll cross that bridge when I get to it," Slocum said, but he'd already thought hard on the matter. He could try to flag down one of the trains and send a message back to David Collingswood about the hiding place. The vice president had the resources to get a dozen men out here inside a day or two and recover the stolen shipment. Or Jackson's part of it.

Slocum wasn't sure what the map actually meant. If Jackson had double-crossed his partners and taken their shares, this might be the entire pile of stolen silver. His mind drifted as he stared at Tamara's back and watched her gently bounce along ahead of him. It was a shame she had been such an important part of the robbery, but he wasn't inclined to let her go scot-free. He had been hired to do a job. Collingswood wasn't paying him to bring in only those in the gang he thought were guilty.

The same problem gnawed at him about Tamara as it had with Jackson. Proof for a jury was hard to come by. Tamara had confessed to him, but it came down to his word against hers. Slocum shrugged that off. The railroad vice president would have to decide, but Slocum wasn't inclined to let him question the woman the way he would have Jackson or any other in the gang. That wouldn't be right.

"How far?" She craned around to look at him. A ray of light caught her face and lit it like he had seen in a painting of an angel. But her beauty and seeming innocence couldn't deter him.

"Are there three trees around a clearing with a rock in the center?"

"I suppose," she said skeptically. "That about describes every clearing in these parts."

He rode closer and looked past her.

He hated to admit how right she was. From the map, this might be the spot. Three tall trees positioned just right, a boulder the size of a cow, and grass all around. Slocum swung down and walked to the rock. From the map, lining it up with one tree and a distant peak ought to give the proper spot. He began hunting for any ground that had been freshly turned.

Tamara rode closer and then began to circle the area.

"Are you sure you read the map right?" She shook her head. "I don't see any sign anyone's been here. No trampled grass, no dug-up ground. Nothing."

Slocum had to agree. He looked for traces beyond the obvious. The spots of cropped grass showed no sign of a horse grazing there in the last couple weeks. He found deer tracks. If Jackson had spent any time here, his horse would have feasted on the ankle-high succulent grass just as the deer had, cropping close to the ground. A horse would have left much more of a stub than a deer, so only deer had come this way.

Giving up for the moment, Slocum sat on the rock and stared in the direction of the tree-mountain alignment.

"Maybe the silver is buried in the other direction. Jack got confused a lot."

Slocum spun around on the rock and studied the terrain. He saw nothing to show this was the hiding place depicted on the map.

"What do we do?" Tamara asked after she had completed her own hunt. "There might be another clearing that looks like this."

Slocum studied the mountains, the peaks Jackson had used as markers, and finally had to admit defeat.

"This is like all the other treasure maps. I can sell it for more than the worth of any treasure."

"I've heard fake maps for valuable mines are sold back East all the time."

"This isn't fake," Slocum said. "Jackson did the map to mark something. I just don't know what it is."

"So what do we do?" Tamara looked at him, a twinkle in her eye. "It's still early. Do you have any idea how we can spend the rest of the day?"

She didn't like it when he told her. They started back for San Francisco right away.

7

Slocum marched Tamara Crittenden down the narrow hall atop the Central California Railroad offices, feeling like a steer in a stockyard chute. He glanced at her desk. Papers had piled up on it during her absence, as if she would return at any moment and efficiently work as David Collingswood's assistant.

"What are you going to say, John?" She looked at him with her bright blue eyes so intense they burned through his soul.

"What I have to." He knocked on the door. When he heard a muffled sound from inside the vice president's office, he took this as permission to enter.

Collingswood sat behind his desk and looked up. A scowl warped his features.

"It's about time you got back."

"I got here as quick as I could," Slocum said. He was startled when Collingswood blinked and stared at him as if he had turned into a pile of hot cow flop. "I brought her straight back. Here's her gun." He slid the Colt New Line across the desk in Collingswood's direction.

The man stared at it as if it would turn into a snake and bite him. Then he pushed it back in Slocum's direction.

"What's going on? You can't just leave like that and not let me know. I have a business to run."

"I was doing my job," Slocum said. Again he got the hot stare. This time he pressed on. "Miss Crittenden told a man named Jackson and his gang about the silver shipment and was supposed to be paid off. Here's what silver I've been able to recover. I got it off Jackson."

"Jackson?"

"Dead in a shoot-out," Slocum said. "I caught Miss Crittenden just after that and tried to find the rest of the shipment."

"What the hell is going on?"

"I'm trying to tell you," Slocum said, getting angry. "She gave the robbers the information about the shipment. The gang's leader was named Jackson, and he tried to double-cross her. Or from what Jackson said, she wanted more when she heard how much had been stolen."

"I'm not talking to you. Tamara, what's this all about?"

"I don't know, sir. Mr. Slocum is confused as to what went on."

"I don't give a rat's ass what he thinks. Where did you go?"

Slocum started to talk, then clamped his mouth shut. He hadn't expected Collingswood to react this way. If anything, Slocum had been working up a fine speech during their ride back to San Francisco asking the railroad vice president to show some clemency for the woman.

"He's right about Jackson. He was one of the robbers. I found out about him but couldn't let anyone know. I had to keep him in sight, and he led me across the Bay and then along the tracks toward where he had robbed the train. I thought he would show me where he had hidden the silver, but I never got the chance to find out. Mr. Slocum made sure of that."

"You shouldn't have risked your life like that," Collingswood said.

"I'm sorry, sir. If Jackson had crossed over to Berkeley without me going after him immediately, he would have disappeared and with him any chance of getting the silver back. I had no chance to let you know. There aren't telegraph stations along that route."

"Only at the depots," Collingswood said. "You shouldn't have gone after this Jackson fellow. I could have had a dozen men on his trail within hours."

"I could have telegraphed from our depot in Oakland," she said contritely. She looked sideways at Slocum. A tiny smile crept to her lips and ran away quickly. "I know that now, sir. I was caught up in the moment and didn't think."

"That's not like you at all. I am disappointed, Tamara."

"She told the owlhoots which train to rob!"

"Slocum, I have no idea what is going on. You said you killed Jackson. Are you sure you didn't let him slip through your fingers and thought—wrongly, I say—to accuse Miss Crittenden for your incompetence?"

"She confessed to me that she gave them the information. How else could they have known which train to rob?"

"Do you have any proof? Other than your word that she, for whatever reason, confessed to you?"

"She's guilty," Slocum said doggedly.

"Her word against yours. Which of you should I believe?" David Collingswood stood and leaned on his desk. Storm clouds swirled about him and turned him dark with anger. "You're fired, Slocum. Get the hell out of here. If you ever show your face in this office or on any other Central California Railroad property, I'll see that you are properly taken care of."

Slocum heaved Jackson's saddlebags up and dropped them onto the desk with a loud thud. He doubted more than fifty dollars in silver rested there, all scraped off the bars in the shipment, but it proved some of his story. It had been

Tamara's payoff. Collingswood grabbed the bags and sent them flying to crash against the wall.

"Get out, Slocum. I swear, if I hear of you ever again, I'll have every policeman in San Francisco down on your neck. And if those worthless louts cannot deal with you, the company specials will."

"Mr. Underwood is a very dangerous man," Tamara said in a low voice that only Slocum heard. Collingswood had taken to shouting and was lost in his own world of outrage.

"You owe me the rest of the month's salary," Slocum said.

"Get out! Out!" Collingswood grabbed for Tamara's pistol, then froze when he saw how Slocum turned to square off. There was no question who would raise his pistol first and fire. "Get out!"

Slocum saw that the railroad man wasn't going to try to shoot him down. If Collingswood did attempt to gun him down, it would be when he turned his back. Slocum stepped away, keeping his eyes on Collingswood. He didn't bother looking in Tamara's direction. She had won without firing a shot or hardly saying a word. Slocum knew this was how it would have gone if she had been brought to trial. Evidence against her was thinner than hair on a bald man's head.

He left the office but didn't bother closing the door.

"I'm sorry this happened, Mr. Collingswood."

"Your work has piled up. Get to it. And find Underwood. I need to send out more specials."

"Yes, sir."

Slocum heard muffled words but no longer found himself interested in what went on in the Central California Railroad office. He stormed past the guard in the lobby, who called out a good-bye. It would be a cold day in hell before Jason had a chance to speak to him again. Once out in the bright, clear San Francisco day, Slocum cooled off a little. But his anger smoldered like embers. He didn't mind that Collingswood saw fit not to bring charges against Tamara. What chapped him most was Collingswood not believing him. If anything, the man had come right out and called him a liar.

He turned and stared at the Central California Railroad building. His hand hovered above his pistol, then he relaxed. Shooting the place up solved nothing. His heated anger turned colder. Slocum walked away, knowing it wasn't worth his bother carrying this any further. More than once he'd been fired from a job, but never for being a liar. That festered in his gut as he went down to Meigg's Wharf and hunted for a rough-and-tumble saloon. He didn't have to look far. Not a one of them was a reputable place where a man could drink without being in fearsome danger, either for his life or for getting shanghaied.

Slocum dropped a dime on the bar.

"Beer," he said.

The barkeep peered at him through his one good eye. The bad one was filmed over and wandered about at will.

"We don't serve piss here. Whiskey or nothing."

"Whiskey, then." Slocum grabbed the man's brawny wrist and forced him to lift the bottle and put it on the bar. "I don't drink alone. You first. I'll pay for it."

The barkeep grunted and pulled free.

"If you're payin', then I want the good stuff." He found a second half-filled bottle under the bar. "Show me the color of your money."

Slocum dropped a silver dollar on the bar. The barkeep picked it up, peered closely at it, hefted it, and then tucked it away in his canvas apron pocket before getting a second shot glass. He poured two stiff drinks. Slocum waited for the man to down his before sampling. He almost gagged.

"This is the good stuff?"

"Better 'n that," he said, pointing at the other bottle. The barkeep laughed harshly. "'Course, you drink that and you end up drinkin' ship's rum for a couple years."

Slocum had guessed right about the first bottle being drugged. He looked into the mirror behind the bar and saw two sailors arguing. One pointed at Slocum, then the other knocked his hand down to the table for being so obvious.

"What's the going rate for a landlubber these days?"

"For you, ten dollars. For most of the derelicts who wash up onshore here, two or maybe three. Not more 'n that."

"Then those two will be pissed something fierce at being robbed," Slocum said. He took a second swig straight from the bottle, spun, and kicked the first sailor in the crotch as he rushed up.

Using the bottle as a club, Slocum smashed it against the second salt's head. The man had a skull made from pure oak. The glass showered down, mixed with the whiskey, and it never fazed him. He crashed into Slocum. Then it was Slocum's turn to get hit over the head. The barkeep swung a cosh with more enthusiasm than skill. His bad eye might have caused him to miss a square blow. It still staggered Slocum.

Slocum let out a roar and stumbled from the bar. The sailor pursued, thinking he had himself another shanghaiing victim. He doubled over when Slocum unloaded a punch that buried itself wrist-deep in his belly. By now a halfdozen others in the saloon joined the fight. They didn't care whose side they were on. They just wanted a good fight.

That was why Slocum had come here. He wanted to vent some steam, and pounding heads and bellies with his fists did just that. Solid punches landed, but Slocum never felt them. He was too intent on landing a jab or haymaker on anonymous brawlers. But when he reared back to unload a punch squarely into a sailor's ugly face, he found his right arm caught in a vise grip he couldn't shake free.

He strained and began to lose footing on the sawdust covering the floor. Still exerting himself, he swiveled around so his face was only inches away from one he knew all too well.

"Underwood!"

"Now, boy, don't get your dander up. The proprietor of

this here place wants more than one customer left in drinkin' condition."

Slocum relaxed, then ducked as Underwood swung his mutilated fist. The bony fingers wrapped up into a tight ball whizzed past Slocum's head and landed smack in the middle of another patron's face. The man stumbled back, was caught by another fighter, and resumed the fray there, not caring whom he swung at.

"Come along now." Underwood caught Slocum by the elbow and lifted slightly.

To his surprise, Slocum couldn't break free of the two-fingered grip. He popped out of the smoky saloon and into the salt air blowing cold and fresh off the Pacific. Only when they were a dozen yards from the saloon did Underwood release him. Slocum stumbled a step and swung about.

"Don't go reachin' for that hogleg," Underwood warned. He stood without any weapon in his hand, but Slocum had worked off most of his outrage and stood with his hands loose at his sides.

"What's Collingswood want from me?" Slocum demanded.

"Damned if I know. My guess is nothin' other than never seein' you again. You riled him up more 'n I've seen since he heard of the robbery."

"I only did what he hired me to do."

"So I hear, so I hear." Underwood made no attempt to grab Slocum's elbow again. Instead he pointed along the two-thousand-foot pier. Without waiting, he set off.

Slocum caught up.

"It wasn't an accident you came after me."

"Could be, since that's my waterin' hole. My port when I'm in port."

"Could be that's an outright lie."

Underwood took no offense. He grinned crookedly and said, "You got me pegged, Slocum. You got me all figured out, haven't you?"

"Why?"

"Well now, let's say that a man can have many masters. Mr. Collingswood, now, he's just one of those I work for. Another of my bosses sent me along to reason with you."

Slocum stayed silent. Underwood would get around to what he had to say eventually. Until then, Slocum let cold calm settle on him. He had been inclined to punch Collingswood in the face, but the fight in the saloon had drained him of the need to do so. It was time to move on. Underwood was only holding him back. After all, he had a few dollars left and rode a horse. It belonged to the Central California Railroad, but Collingswood owed him for half the promised wages. Fifty dollars for the nag was outrageous, but he had tack along with it. He was willing to call the debt even with the railroad.

"You don't care to know who that is? Or do you know?"

Since he knew so few people in town, it took him less than a second to work it out.

"She wants my scalp for turning her over to Collingswood." He made it a flat statement.

"You are quick on the uptake. I like that about you. Yes, sir, Tamara Crittenden sees the same in you. Maybe a bit more, her being the way she is."

"What way's that?"

Underwood laughed.

"Horny as all get-out. I never saw a woman so driven. I'd say she was one of them there nymphomaniacs, only it ain't always sex she wants. She gets it into her purty li'l head she wants something and no price is too big. Son, I think she wants you."

"Is that how she pays you?"

"I wish it was. She's too selective, and there's nothin' much I can get her, leastways like that. I lost more 'n my fingers in that fall." Underwood stopped. Slocum went a few steps farther before he realized the man wasn't keeping pace. Underwood pointed using his good finger. "There. That building. You go right on up the stairs to the second floor. There's only one door at the landing. I don't reckon she expects you to knock, but she surely does expect you."

Underwood gave him a one-fingered salute and turned back down the wharf, not looking back to see what Slocum did.

Slocum considered all the things he might do, then went to the stairs and climbed them slowly. He made sure he didn't announce his coming, but before he knocked, he heard Tamara call from inside, "The door's open, John. Come in."

He pushed it open with his toe, expecting to be greeted with a shotgun blast. If she wanted to make him suffer, she'd put a few rounds from her .22 into him. He had no idea what he expected he was walking into. Seeing her seated at a table with a few papers spread in front of her wasn't it.

"You're letting the breeze in. I'm a bit chilly."

"That's not the way you look to me," he said, stepping in and kicking the door shut with the side of his boot.

A quick look around showed nothing for him to be wary of, unless it was the woman seated at the table. She had changed from her trail clothes into a simple dress with a neckline that plunged down far enough to expose the tops of her breasts. Her waist was small and cinched in with a broad leather belt. The table hid her lower half until she stood and came around it. She padded barefoot to him.

Tamara looked up at him, her body pressed close to him. He kept his hands hanging at his sides, as much as he wanted to circle her waist and draw her even closer. A coral snake was lovely, but woe to anyone trying to touch it.

"I'm glad Underwood found you so fast." She reached up and lightly touched a cut on his cheek. "I thought you'd find a fight since you didn't punch out Mr. Collingswood. You have the mad worked out of your system?"

"I have the horse and saddle I got over at the Oakland depot. That's enough pay for my time, that and what few dollars I have left. Since I was flat broke busted when I came to San Francisco, I'm ahead of the game."

"Money, horse, tack," she said, nodding. This caused some of her raven-dark hair to come loose and fall across her left eye. She made no move to push it back. Slocum did it for her.

"You aren't mad at me for turning you over to Collingswood?"

"Mad? Not really. It surprised me, I have to admit." She pressed a bit closer. He felt her hot breath against his throat and the beating of her heart through her breast and thin dress. "It is almost impossible to find a man with such integrity."

"I worked for the railroad. I gave my word."

"That's what makes you so different. Too many men see a promise made as a sometime thing."

"I don't work for the railroad any longer."

"No duty owed to either Mr. Collingswood or the Central California Railroad," she said. "You aren't beholden to them anymore?"

Slocum put his hands around her slender waist. He felt the heat from her body. It matched his own.

"Not a bit. What about you? You still have your job."

"I never promised to find the silver or make sure it ended up in the bank vault owned by the railroad."

"Do tell," he said. He pulled her closer until they both gasped for breath.

"I want someone who can give me his word, and I'll know he can keep it."

"Unlike Jackson."

"We can work together."

"Can I trust your word?"

"We can spit in our palms and shake on it," she said.

"That's not good enough. I know you're a crook."

"What more can I do to show you I can keep my word if we agree to be partners? What can seal the contract?"

Slocum caught his breath as her hand wormed its way

between their tightly pressed bodies and began inching down from his chest to his belly, and then even lower until she gripped the growing bulge at his crotch.

For his part, Slocum moved his hands around her waist, then down until he cupped her buttocks. They were firm and not what he had expected, although he had seen how easily she rode. When she began grinding herself against him, he felt growing discomfort.

"I understand," she said. "Some things need to be free." She unfastened his gun belt and dropped it to the floor. She moved down so she knelt in front of him.

Her quick fingers unfastened his fly, the buttons popping like gunfire as each slid free. She reached into the darkness and fumbled a bit, finally pulling him from his cloth prison. For a moment, Slocum realized what she had meant about a chill in the air. Then he gasped. The wind blowing across his heated organ disappeared as she took him fully into her mouth. He felt the bulbous end of his manhood slide along her tender inner cheek, then dive deeper down her throat. When she swallowed, he almost lost control like a young buck with his first woman.

Slocum laced his fingers through her lustrous hair and pulled her away gently. As he slid from between her lips, she treated him to a rough tonguing and teeth that gently dug into his tender flesh. When only the purpled knob remained between her lips, he paused to garner his strength. She almost robbed him of control again when she squeezed the hairy sac dangling beneath his shaft and began sucking with a vengeance.

Stroking, licking, sucking, she moved back and forth along his length until he turned weak in the knees. He stroked over her hair, wondering if he dared seal the deal then and there. But that wouldn't be fair to Tamara—and he wanted more.

Insistent, he pulled her away from his groin so she could look up. The wicked smile on her lips would have been enough goad for him, but she whispered in a husky voice, "I'm wet. Take me, John. Take me now."

He reached under her arms and lifted her easily into the air. Her legs scissored apart and circled his waist so she locked her heels behind his back. Billows of skirt separated him from his target. He walked forward two paces and set her on the edge of the table. Tamara leaned back, supporting herself on her elbows. Her eyes sparkled, and her face was flushed. He saw her arousal spreading from her cheeks to her throat and gracing the upper slopes of her breasts. Her breath came in sharper pants now.

Working his hands under her, he pulled away her skirt and found she wore nothing beneath. His fingers slipped along the liquid gash between her legs. A shudder passed through her as she sank back flat on the table. Her knees rose on either side of him.

"Don't stop, don't stop. I need it. I need *you!*"

He dipped a finger into her heated well, then smeared the thick womanly oils all about before moving closer. The tip of his shaft slipped along her nether lips. A few strokes caused her to shut her eyes and clench down hard at the sides of the table. When he felt as if he was going to explode like a stick of dynamite, he pulled her closer. For an instant, the bones in his legs melted. He sank balls deep in her moist, hot center.

Surrounded by the female sheath, he found himself unable to move. He let the heat seep into his dick. Then he began moving his hips, not in and out but in a circular motion that stirred him around inside her. She gasped and began moaning. Words failed to form. Her ass lifted off the table, and she crammed herself down harder against him. He sank in a fraction of an inch more, but this was enough to ignite his passions.

He withdrew slowly, relishing every inch of the retreat. Then he slammed hard into her, lifting her from the table again. She kicked out so her legs were straight on either side of him. This gave a new and deliciously wicked sensation that boiled about in his loins. She locked her heels behind him again to keep him from pulling out.

With a slow motion, he stirred about again, his manhood a spoon in her mixing bowl. Tamara began moving in the opposite direction, adding to their arousal. When her heels slipped behind him, he withdrew and began thrusting. The movement was slow at first, then built speed like a locomotive going up a steep grade. When he hit the top of the grade, he raced in and out of her.

In the distance he heard her cry out as waves of desire broke over her. His ears were filled with the hammering of his own heart. He gripped her hips and pulled her more firmly into him with every pistoning stoke until his steel turned to a skyrocket. And then, all too soon, he melted within her. Sweat poured down his face and into his eyes. He tossed his head to one side and got rid of some of the perspiration.

She lay spread on the table before him, complete pleasure glowing in every line on her face.

"Admit it, that's so much better than a handshake," she said.

"The deal's only half-approved," he said.

"Are you man enough to complete the contract?" she asked.

"I promise."

He bent low and kissed her. It took a spell but their partnership was mutually signed, sealed, and delightfully delivered before nightfall.

8

"How did you meet Jackson?"

Slocum lounged back on Tamara's narrow bed, watching her closely.

She made no effort to hide her nakedness as she dressed. It was as if she performed for an audience. In a way, she did. It was an audience of one, and he was appreciative. A daringly exposed thigh vanished as she pulled up her skirt and worked to fasten it at her trim waist. She pirouetted carefully so he got a full view of her nakedness above the waist. Tamara stopped when her back was to him and climbed slowly into her blouse. A shrug or two settled the garment but also gave her breasts a delightful jiggle that made Slocum hard again—almost. They had expended the full measure of their passion with the first lovemaking. Then they had retired to her bed and explored each other until both were ready again.

But even as it exhausted Slocum sexually, it had rekindled his curiosity about her and Jackson.

She finished the last button and turned. For a moment the western sun slanted through the window and gave her dark hair golden highlights. Another small turn let the rays catch the pearl buttons on her blouse. It looked as if a string of golden nuggets pointed downward where Slocum had just visited.

"I don't remember."

"Was he someone Underwood brought in for a job?"

"Oh, no, Underwood didn't start doing that until after the robbery. I knew him from . . . earlier."

"You worked in a saloon?"

This brought a peal of laughter ringing forth. She sat on the edge of the bed, her warm hand against his bare chest. With a small gesture, she curled her fingers downward so the nails cut into his flesh.

"Do you think I could ever be a barroom floozy? A cheap whore?"

From the grip she had on him, a wrong answer would result in painful scratches.

"You play the game on so many different levels, it's hard to say. You're not only clever, you're beautiful." He kept her from scratching him as he sat up and gave her a kiss.

"And I thought I was the only one who used sex to get what I want," she said, shaking her head. "You are quite the Lothario, John Slocum."

"I don't know who that is, but if you're interested in him, point him out."

She laughed delightedly.

"One of the many things I like about you is that I can never tell when you are joking." Before he could pull her back down for another kiss, she disengaged and slipped away to sit at the table. She hiked up a foot and braced it on the edge of the table, exposing herself all the way to the crotch. "I need help with my shoes. They are so hard to button."

He swung around and reached for his pants.

"Oh, no, don't dress. Come here and put on my shoes."

He considered for a moment, then went to her. Dropping

to his knees, he stroked up her leg, paused at her inner thigh, then moved higher. She gasped as his finger entered her. When she closed her eyes and pleasure began to take over her features, he backed away.

Her foot fell heavily to the floor as his unexpected departure unbalanced her.

"You're a big girl. Put on your own shoes."

A moment's anger flashed on her face, then she smiled ruefully. "As long as you promise to undress me again later."

He pulled on his longjohns, climbed into his jeans, and worked to get shirt, vest, and coat on. When he strapped on his gun belt, he felt dressed—or as dressed as Tamara. She remained barefoot and so did he.

"How did you meet Jackson?"

She sighed in resignation and began working her feet into her tight shoes.

"At the bank over on Market. I had to post a payroll for the office workers and saw him loitering about. Mr. Collingswood had hired me a few weeks earlier, and the temptation of stealing so much silver from a Virginia City shipment had burned itself into my imagination. I could get the information but had no way of acting on it."

"Jackson was casing the bank?"

"I thought so. He never said as I approached him, but he had the look of a real desperado."

"You convinced him to forget the bank and rob the train?"

"It took very little persuasion. I told him of the huge amounts of silver shipped from Virginia City but had no idea how much would be in the shipment he and his gang stole."

"He's not going to tell us about the silver. Who are the other three in the gang?"

"I don't know. He had already recruited them for the bank robbery and only went in himself to be sure when there'd be the most money in the vault. I never saw them, much less met them."

Slocum pulled on his boots, turning over each detail in his head. He settled his feet securely, then leaned back in the chair, watching as Tamara buttoned her shoes. She bent over, exposing the tops of her breasts. Forcing himself to think about the stolen silver rather than her took some willpower.

This sparked caution in him. She could kill a man as easily as he could, only her weapon was softer.

"It's safe to say he didn't frequent the Union Club."

"Mr. Collingswood does, but you're right, Jack would have been more at home along the Barbary Coast."

"That's where I'll start looking for the others in his gang," Slocum said, standing. Tamara shot to her feet and started to leave. He took her arm and swung her about. "I'll go alone. If you showed your face in the Barbary dives, there'd be more trouble than information gathered."

"Take Underwood, then. You need someone to watch your back."

Slocum trusted Underwood as far as he could throw him, but he refrained from telling her. He had the feeling she and the two-fingered man were closer to being partners than he was with her.

"Can you use that pistol you carry?"

"Of course I can. I can shoot the eye out of a rat at ten paces."

"Where we're going, there'll be a lot of rats, none of them four-legged."

She smiled wickedly, as if the idea of killing someone pleased her. She fetched her Colt New Line, checked the cylinder to be sure it carried all seven rounds. She held up the octagonal-barreled weapon so it pointed at the ceiling and struck a pose, her other hand balled and resting on a cocked hip.

"I'm ready."

"Put the gun away where nobody can see it, but you can get to it." He waited for her to slip it into a pocket in her skirt. "You might keep your hand on it, but don't put a finger on the trigger until you have it aimed at someone you want to kill."

"I won't shoot myself, John. You worry so." She gave him a light kiss on the cheek.

He wondered if she had ever shot anyone with the pistol. Or had she killed someone? She was a vision of loveliness, but it was the same deadly beauty he found in diamondback rattlesnakes: sinuous and harmless unless provoked.

The sun sank into the Pacific Ocean just beyond the Golden Gate. Slocum stopped and watched as either side of the portal into San Francisco Bay turned from natural to metallic. Chiu Jin Shan—the Old Gold Mountain, the Chinese called it. The sun vanished completely, and a chill wind picked up off the harbor, bringing with it the smell of floating garbage and rotten fish.

Slocum told himself the hunt for Jackson's partners could turn from golden to deadly as quickly as the sun disappeared. The laborers along the Embarcadero finished the last of their chores and drifted away to the bars. He tried to imagine where a man like Jackson would wet his whistle. Not with the sailors. Jackson was a landlubber, and unless he saw a reason to frequent the seamen's dives, he would keep away from the waterfront.

"Where do the men drink who aren't sailors or stevedores?"

"Underwood would know. Don't you trust him?"

"I have no reason to. If he gets involved in this, he has to choose between two masters." Slocum considered this, then amended, "Between Collingswood as his master and you as his mistress."

"Why, John, I'd never be *his* mistress."

Slocum knew Tamara could get Underwood to jump around like a flea on a hot griddle, because she so easily did that with everyone else in her life. David Collingswood would believe her to be loyal despite strong evidence to the contrary, even if Slocum hadn't provided much more than his observations as proof of her part in the robbery. Jackson had gone along with her when he likely preferred robbing a bank to a train. And Slocum knew he had to be careful not to fall under her spell. To do so might mean his life.

Right now he preferred to find the silver and ride off with it because of the way Collingswood had treated him. The railroad owed him for not trusting him when he had given his word. And the railroad vice president had come right out and called him a liar without examining the evidence.

Such an insult had to be met with the proper punishment. Slocum heard desperation in Collingswood's every word and knew the higher-ups in the Central California Railroad would fire their vice president in a heartbeat if the silver wasn't recovered. Or did they even know? Collingswood had gone out of his way to keep the theft quiet. Sending out an army of specials was risky, giving more credence to Slocum's guess that quick recovery would be more than appreciated—it had to be necessary to keep Collingswood's head from getting chopped off.

Depending on the president of the railroad and his directors, that might be an actual description. Collingswood might not be fired but instead be left floating facedown in the Bay.

"What are you thinking, John?"

"There are saloons down around Mission Dolores. That's where a man riding into town from the south would spot a watering hole. Drovers and other cowboys coming to town would ride in there."

"I am sure Jack wasn't a sailor, but he never said anything about being a wrangler either." She caught on to what Slocum was saying. "He doesn't have to be a cowboy. He could be a stagecoach robber or anything else on the other side of the law, but he would ride in and find cowboys more to his liking."

"If Jackson had ever been to San Francisco before, he'd

know how dangerous it was for anyone to drink along the Barbary Coast."

"Good thinking, John, but this town is filled with gin mills. How do you find the right one? And how do you ask after the rest of his gang?"

"It's about time we had some luck."

Slocum knew they'd need more than some. They'd need a passel. He got it after downing almost a full bottle of whiskey one shot at a time.

His vision blurred from too much cheap whiskey. Even tossing more than one shot onto the floor of each drinking emporium where he lingered took away only a small portion of his inebriation. Tamara chided him constantly, but Slocum knew if he didn't knock back a shot or two when he was being watched by everyone in each saloon, he would find out nothing. Until he came to Lead Bottom's Saloon, all he had to show for his diligence was a head that threatened to explode and a belly that churned like the storm-tossed Pacific.

But his patience finally paid off. He stared at three men playing poker. Two were in cahoots cleaning out the third. The sucker had no idea how he was being hoodwinked because the two worked together so expertly. The pair let him win a few small pots and took the bigger ones by signaling each other and, twice that Slocum saw, trading cards. What caught his eye was the way the sucker bet.

He used small silver bars instead of cartwheels or greenbacks. He had begun with a half dozen and had only two left. Slocum wanted to get a better look. To do that meant he had to be in the game.

"Mind if I sit in?" He dropped his paltry few dollars onto the poker table, then sat down without waiting for an invitation, glad to take the load off his aching legs. He wobbled just a bit, and not all of it was show to let the two working in tandem know he was an easy mark, too. Even so, they started to object. They needed to win only two more of the silver bars to finish cleaning out the man next to Slocum.

"We got a private game, mister," said one of the cheats.

"Aw, let 'im set in. We can use fresh blood. I need a player I can whomp up on 'fore you gents take me for every last cent I have."

"Thanks," Slocum said. He eyed the silver bars. The other two weren't likely to put up the ones they had already won since they had piles of scrip and smaller coins.

He played carefully for a couple hands, worrying that the man with the silver bars would lose. The two let him and Slocum win a few pots. Seeing how they cheated gave Slocum a good idea how to win. When he was dealt two pair, jacks and queens, any reasonable man would draw one. Instead, he threw away the jacks and dross card. From the way the man dealing acted, Slocum knew he had done the right thing. He cleared his throat and stared hard at the man.

"Deal. Fair and square. Off the top." Slocum forced the man's hand down so he had to give him the first three cards.

Slocum glanced at his hand. Three aces, two queens, full house. Even better, they had set up the gent with the silver, giving him a full house, too. The fourth ace likely rested in the one's hand who should have received the triplet of aces.

"I can't let the best hand o' the night go to waste," the man said. "Here. I'm puttin' in both bars."

Slocum saw the anger building on the other men's faces and knew who had the best hand. He pushed in all his money, including the small winnings from earlier pots.

"Got to call you."

Both the men folded, leaving Slocum in the pot with the suspected train robber.

"You have to beat tens full of kings." The man beamed proudly as he laid down the cards.

"I've a better spread," Slocum said. He shifted to get his gun hand over near the ebony butt of his Colt in case anyone disputed the cards.

To his surprise, no one did. The two gamblers grumbled about their own bad luck, and the man who had lost both silver bars laughed, scratched himself, and declared, "Damn my bad luck. As if it wasn't bad enough losing to them, I got to lose to you, too. That cleans me out."

"You're taking it mighty well," Slocum said, but he watched the other two.

"It's only money. I can get more, whenever I want."

"It must be nice to be rich," Slocum said.

This sparked caution. The sallow man realized he had said too much.

"I got a rich uncle, that's all. Come next month, yeah, next month, he'll give me more."

Slocum picked up a silver bar and looked at it. From the description David Collingswood had given him, this was one of the bars stolen from the Central California Railroad.

"Least I can do, cleaning you out like that, is to buy you a drink." Slocum wanted to loosen the robber's tongue. Otherwise, finding the remainder of the stolen silver could be a drawn-out quest.

"Had enough for the night. I'll want a chance to win back my silver some other time, gents." The robber got to his feet and left before Slocum could even stand.

When he did get his shaky legs under him, a strong hand grabbed his wrist and pulled him back down. He sat heavily and pulled free. He locked eyes with the gambler next to him.

"We were the big winners. Let us buy you a round."

"He had the right idea. Time to grab some sleep and—"

"You refusin' to drink with us? We ain't good enough for you?"

"Who am I to turn down a free drink?" Slocum said, but he seethed at the delay. He hoped Tamara had enough sense to follow the train robber—losing the man now would make for more difficult tracking later. He had gotten lucky noticing the silver in the poker game. Even better luck would be finding where the robber had stashed his share of the silver.

"Hey, Lead Bottom, bring us a round," the gambler who hadn't spoken so far bellowed. "The special bottle."

Slocum tensed at this. Every drinking emporium along the Embarcadero had a "special" bottle laced with Mickey Finns. The chloral hydrate knocked out the fool swilling it to make him easy prey for the shanghaiers. They were a mile from the docks and farther from the ships gently wallowing at anchor in the Bay, but that didn't mean the knockout drops weren't available here, too, south of town where cowboys rather than sailors drank.

The barkeep came from behind the long plank propped up on two sawhorses. Slocum almost laughed. Lead Bottom's jeans hung slack in the backside.

"I got my butt shot off," the barkeep said, seeing Slocum's reaction. "I still got a half pound of lead in me. Don't take kindly to anyone makin' light of my affliction."

Slocum almost knocked back the drink set before him to stifle a comeback. There weren't many men who told the truth about such things. Lead Bottom might have sat on a hot stove and done the damage to himself as easily as getting in a colorful gunfight and being first the hero and then the victim.

"Drink up," the nearer gambler said.

Slocum saw how both men sat, one hand under the table. His attention had strayed as he thought on the barkeep's predicament. That gave both of his adversaries the chance to slip out pistols. If he failed to drink, they would cut him in half before he could reach his own six-shooter.

"Bottoms up," Slocum said, upending the glass and letting the burning fluid slip smoothly into his mouth.

9

Slocum swilled the liquor around in his mouth. His eyes went wide, and he fell facedown onto the poker table. Chips and money went skittering away as he slid off and fell onto the floor.

"Damnation, never seen anybody knocked out that fast," Lead Bottom said.

"Keep yer damn hands off the silver," growled the gambler who had been next to Slocum. "That's ours."

"You owe me a cut. You ain't been payin' up like you should have been. I seen how you varmints steal from my best customers."

The three men argued for a spell, then one gambler kicked Slocum in the ribs.

"Why'd you do that for?" The barkeep sounded genuinely perplexed. "He ain't goin' nowhere. That's 'bout the most powerfulest Mickey in the whole of Frisco."

"Just checkin'. You got our winnin's, Joe Bob?"

"All tucked away," said the other gambler.

"My cut," said the bartender. "You owe me my cut fer tonight and all of last week. You cleaned out two of them railroad men what stopped in here. I remember it plain as day."

"What do you want?"

"One of them silver bars ought to do it."

They haggled a bit more, then Lead Bottom subsided.

"You're a crook," a gambler said.

The barkeep laughed and said, "You should talk. Them's the slickest, fastest fingers I ever saw deal a second."

"If you could see it, I'd be a mighty poor dealer."

"Come on, Joe Bob. We want to see what the action's like over at the Lost Virtue."

Slocum opened his eyes just enough to see two pairs of boots scooting across the floor and then vanish through the door. A cool blast of air hit him in the face, but he didn't need it to revive himself. He hadn't swallowed and, when he hit the floor, had spit out the doctored whiskey. What giddiness he felt came from all the drinking he had done earlier.

When Lead Bottom grunted, reached under his arms to heave him to his feet, the barkeep got the surprise of his life. Slocum surged upward, stared the startled man in the eye, then delivered a short punch that ended on the man's temple. The bartender's eyes rolled up in his head, and he collapsed to the spot where Slocum had lain only seconds before.

Slocum resisted the urge to deliver a kick to the man's ribs. His own ribs hurt, but it had been the gambler named Joe Bob who had assaulted what he thought was an unconscious man. With a deft grab, he took the silver bar from the bartender, then scrounged around and found what money had been missed by the departing gamblers. They were as efficient in their hunt for loose change as they had been in fleecing the train robber.

With the bar weighing down his coat pocket, Slocum stepped out into the dawn and looked around for Tamara. Not finding her meant nothing. If she had any sense, she followed the train robber. He walked along the dusty street and found himself heading south for no good reason.

Slocum stopped and let the cold morning air clear his head of the last cobwebs draped over his brain.

He thought about possible places the robber might head. The robber had been cleaned out but wasn't worried. He had a mountain of silver stashed somewhere, but was it nearby? Slocum doubted that. Still, he must have a horse stabled nearby. Slocum fetched his, noting that Tamara's wasn't hitched up alongside anymore. He snapped the reins and got the mare ambling along. When a merchant stuck his head out to see if he had a customer so early in the morning, Slocum called out, "Where's the livery stable?"

"Down the street. Keep riding another quarter mile or so. It's the only one in town, but my boy's a good farrier. If you need a shoe put on, he can do it for half what that thief Farnum'd charge."

"Much obliged." Slocum picked up the pace and found the stables easily. The smithy already had his forge hot and hammered away at what looked to be a crowbar.

"You in the market for some good ironwork?" The smithy held up the red-glowing crowbar almost hammered into workable shape. "I can fix you up with anything you need after I finish this off for the railroad. Rush job."

"My partner's ahead of me. He said he left his horse with a man named Farnum, about the best blacksmith in these parts. That you?"

"Is."

Slocum saw by the man's expression he had greased the rails for his next question by establishing his bona fides.

"Has Jones already ridden on?"

"Jones? Your partner's named Jones?" Farnum scratched his nose, spat into the fire, then went back to forming the crowbar. "Only one who's rode on out today's named Drury."

"Sorry, I was thinking of our other partner. Drury's about your height, real pale, thin to the point of being a skeleton." Slocum remembered something more that his nose had detected back at Lead Bottom's to keep Farnum from thinking it odd a man didn't know his own partner's name. "He enjoys smoking a bit of opium now and then."

"That's the one," the smithy said, critically examining his work, then quenching it with a loud hiss. "Chasing the dragon's been the ruin of more 'n one man. Them damned Chinee bring in the opium and sell it so cheap a man's sore tempted to smoke instead of drinking booze."

"How long ago did he head south?"

"You're not a half hour behind him. He rode off, a bit out of kilter."

"How's that?"

"Staying in the saddle proved quite a chore. Stepped up onto his stallion just fine, but he got to leanin' to one side and had a devil of a time righting himself. I couldn't tell if it was from smokin' or drinkin'."

Slocum snorted and said, "Both."

"My thoughts." Farnum stared up at him. "You look like a decent sort. Steer clear of him. When a man gets to spendin' time in them opium dens, he's a lost cause."

"Thanks for the advice. Drury needs a bit of salvation in his life, that's all."

"More than a bit, if you ask me."

Slocum touched the brim of his hat and trotted out onto the single road leading south. Drury needed more of the stolen silver if he intended to smoke more opium. Hiding his share of the shipment in San Francisco was foolish. There was so much, he'd need a wagon to cart it in. Better to leave it south or even around the end of San Francisco Bay back in the direction where the robbery had occurred. If Drury rode to meet another of the robbers, so much the better.

Getting the hiding place from Drury would be easy enough but would take time. How much opium would he have to smoke before his tongue loosened? A second outlaw gave double the chance of finding the silver in a hurry. Slocum knew ways of making a man talk, but some took longer than others. And a few men kept their vow to die before revealing a secret. Drury had struck him as the kind to spill his guts right away, but not knowing him put Slocum at a disadvantage.

Keeping a steady pace brought him to the spot in the road where he saw two riders ahead. There had been a few travelers out early in the morning, but they all headed north to San Francisco on obvious business. Two had driven empty wagons but had womenfolk riding beside them in the driver's box. A half-dozen other men had the look of miners hunting for supplies. Slocum knew the golden gleam in their eyes brought by hope and greed. The only ones getting rich off their mining efforts would be the storekeepers selling them their supplies.

The two ahead rode slowly but with some determination. As they turned east when the town of Fremont poked up on the far side of the Bay, Slocum spurred his horse to a gallop. He knew where these two were now. Let them vanish into a town and his job turned more difficult. He had poured too much rotgut down his throat the night before to repeat it anytime soon. More than that, his luck had run good. Flopping up and down at his side, he touched the pocket containing the silver bar. These men could tell him what Jackson hadn't. He was going to be rich. He was going to keep it as payment for Collingswood insulting him, and then he would ride north to Oregon. Buying a spread on the ocean side of the Cascades where he could raise Appaloosas seemed a decent way to spend a few years of his life.

He tried to keep his mare galloping, but the animal was tuckered out and not anywhere near the mount that those Appaloosas he thought on were. The horse began to falter, forcing Slocum to slow and finally come to a complete halt. Better to catch up with the outlaws in Fremont than to have the mare die under him now.

Still, he fumed at being so close and letting the two slip through his fingers like this. Finally settling down, having confidence in his own tracking abilities—and buoyed by the weight of the silver bar in his pocket—he walked slowly into Fremont. Drury and his partner had beat him into town by better than twenty minutes. The sun had risen about halfway up in the brilliant blue sky. When his belly growled from lack of food and being abused with too much whiskey, Slocum considered what the two outlaws might do.

Drury was in no better shape. The newcomer might have wolfed down a big breakfast, but Slocum doubted it. They would head for a saloon serving lunch.

Or a restaurant. Slocum drew rein and stared through the plate glass window of a sizable restaurant. Drury and the other man sat just behind two women at the front table. He jockeyed his horse about to get a better view. It wouldn't do now to mistake his quarry.

He dismounted, intending to go into the restaurant and do what it took to take both of them prisoners. The pitiful whinnying warned him that his horse needed attention first. Slocum pursed his lips and considered his chances of finding both Drury and his partner still eating when he got back. From the way they both shoveled the food from their plates into their pie holes, he thought he had a fair amount of time.

Slocum led his horse to a livery a block off the main street, paid for feed and tending, then returned as the two outlaws finished what looked to be their second servings of peach cobbler.

He went in, took a chair at a small table where he could watch them from the corner of his eye. Drury might remember him as the drunk poker player who had taken his last two silver bars, but Slocum had to take the gamble if he wanted to find the silver they had hidden away.

Sipping at weak coffee did nothing to bolster his strength, but it went a ways to clearing his head. Tackling the two inside the restaurant was foolish when a dozen other customers were working on their food. Bullets flying, the confusion, possibly innocent men and women being shot—any of that attracted the attention of the local marshal. Slocum wanted to avoid that as much as possible. Explaining the situation would land him in jail faster than the men he set upon.

Drury looked pale and jumpy, eyes darting around constantly. Slocum knew the lack of opium wore on him. The only reason he had left San Francisco and the easy access to Chinatown where he could find any number of opium dens had to be lack of money. Even as he thought that, Slocum touched the bulge in his coat pocket and smiled.

The man with Drury was stockier and dressed like a wrangler. From the look of it, he wasn't much of a gunslinger. He wore his six-shooter up high on his hip in a soft leather holster. The man's immense hands about swallowed up the coffee cup as he drained it before setting it down with a loud click.

"We kin go, Drury. You're looked mighty peaked."

"I'm all right, I tell you." The man's twitching hands put that to the lie. "We got to go back to Frisco. Gimme what I want and—"

"No way. You got your share, I got mine. You want dope, you pay for it out of your own cut."

Slocum shifted a little in the chair to bring his hand around to the butt of his Colt. The two had given him all the assurance he needed that they were the train robbers who had worked with Jackson. It had worried him that Drury had stolen the silver bars from the actual train robbers or had come by them honestly. But the skeletal man and his chunky partner were the robbers.

David Collingswood would give a small fortune to have these men in custody. Slocum was after a large fortune. They might not know where Jackson's share was stashed, but between them, they had half the silver.

His attention shifted to a pair of men in the doorway. Both carried rifles in the crooks of their arms. One nudged another and pointed at Drury and his partner.

Slocum swung back to the outlaws in time to see them

going for their six-guns. Then all hell broke loose. Drury fired wildly. His partner proved cooler under fire, in spite of the manner in which he carried his six-shooter. Every shot he got off went directly toward the men in the door.

For their part, they wasted no time swinging their rifles around and firing as wildly as Drury. Shrieks from the customers were drowned out by the steady snap from the rifles. The plate glass window exploded into a thousand shards, and more than one saucer or cup crashed to the floor. From the kitchen the cook ran out, waving a meat cleaver. Slocum tried to shout a warning—too late.

Drury caught the motion from the corner of his eye and made his one accurate shot. The cook stopped, stood up straight, looked curiously at his chest where a red splotch spread, then dropped his cleaver and followed it to the floor. He kicked feebly. Slocum doubted he was dead, but from the twitching, it wouldn't be long.

"Give up, you sons of bitches! You're under arrest!"

The two in the door had ducked back outside and fired past the doorjamb. Drury's partner proved smarter than the men outside, who thought the thin wood walls protected them. He shot through the walls, drilling .45-caliber holes that let in slanting rays of daylight. One slug found its target. The rifleman yelped like a stuck pig and began cursing with increasing imagination. For his part, Slocum whipped out his Colt and tried to get the drop on the outlaws. He was driven down under the table as Drury flung a shot in his direction.

He looked out in time to see the pair of robbers vault over the cook and vanish into the kitchen.

"They's goin' 'round back!" someone yelled. "Head 'em off!"

The two outside stopped filling the restaurant interior with wildly fired bullets and split up, one going in each direction around the building after the outlaws. Slocum considered what to do. It was more dangerous than he preferred, but he couldn't let Drury and his partner escape. He stepped over the cook and chanced a quick look into the kitchen. Both outlaws had fled through the back door.

He took a deep breath and went after them. A quick peek out showed him that the outlaws were gone, but the two who had started the fight were hard on their heels, running down a path toward the outhouse. Slocum pounded after them, only to be seen by one who lagged behind his partner, panting for breath and red in the face. When he saw Slocum, he lifted his rifle and got off a round.

"Harry, there's another of them. He's behind us. They got us trapped 'twixt them, two up front and one behind."

The man levered in another round and got off a shot. The first had missed Slocum by a country mile. The second came disturbingly close. He returned fire more accurately but succeeded only in driving the man to cover behind the privy. Slocum found himself unable to get past to go after Drury without crossing the rifleman's field of fire. He skidded to a halt and tried to spot the men farther along the trail. They had leaped across a small stream and vanished in a wooded area. The other rifleman was nowhere to be seen.

"You grab some sky, mister. Throw down that six-gun of yours, and I won't kill you."

The assurance did nothing to soothe Slocum's ruffled feathers. Every second he wasted let Drury and his partner get that much farther away. He triggered a couple shots through the side of the outhouse and got an aggrieved cry from inside.

"What in tarnation's goin' on? You quit shootin' this second, or I'll clap your worthless carcass in jail."

Slocum cursed when the door opened to a man sitting on the throne inside. A deputy's badge gleamed in the sunlight.

Then the man half stood, pulling up his pants. The slug that tore through the rear outhouse wall caught him in the back of the head. He snapped forward and lay facedown on the ground, half in and half outside the privy.

"You killed a lawman," Slocum shouted. "I'm empowered to take you in for aiding and abetting train robbers. Now I got to arrest you for murder, too." It was a bluff, but he still had the papers Collingswood had given him folded up in his pocket. All he wanted was for the rifleman to hightail it so he could get after the two outlaws.

The rifleman confounded him again by stepping out, rifle leveled.

Slocum sighted in for a killing shot until he felt the hot muzzle of a recently fired rifle press into the back of his head.

"Drop it or I'll blow your damned head off."

10

Slocum didn't drop his Colt but lifted his hands, holding them out level with his shoulders. The man in front of him came into full view from behind the outhouse. He never glanced at the deputy he had shot from behind. He clutched his rifle so hard his hands shook.

"I wanna kill him, Harry. Don't you go blowin' off his head. I wanna do it."

"Shut up, Riley," said the man behind Slocum. "You done enough damage for one day. Did you shoot the deputy?"

"I don't know what . . ." His voice trailed off as he looked around and saw the dead lawman. "Sweet Jesus, it musta been this varmint."

"That's a rifle hole in the back of his skull," Slocum said.

"You shut up." The man behind him poked his back with the rifle.

Slocum shifted slightly to his left and then spun to his right as fast as he could, swinging his pistol around in a broad arc that ended at the man's temple. His target went down to his knees, stunned. Keeping up his spinning motion, Slocum knocked the rifle from the man's hands and then brought his six-shooter up, centered on the deputy killer's heart.

"Don't shoot, mister. Don't! You kilt Harry!"

"He's not dead," Slocum said. "You will be if you don't drop the rifle."

"You mean it when you said you was a lawman?" He carefully placed the rifle on the ground, as if laying an offering on some pagan shrine.

"I was deputized by the Central California Railroad to go after train robbers. That gives me the power to arrest you." This was the last thing Slocum wanted to do. Drury was skedaddling away with the location of the stolen silver locked in his head. Every minute he ran put him that much farther from Slocum getting to be a rich man.

"Fancy that," Riley said. "Me and Harry are, too. We got papers from Mr. Collingswood up in that fancy office on top of a big San Francisco building. You want to see?" He started to reach into his coat pocket. Slocum cocked his pistol, ready to shoot.

"W-wait," came Harry's weak voice. "You buffaloed me good and proper, but you don't have to kill Riley. He's not always right in the head."

"You really work for the Central California Railroad?" Slocum asked.

"Yup, the both of us." Harry pressed his hand against the cut on his scalp oozing blood. "Who recruited you?"

Slocum knew his chances of finding Drury were sinking fast. Enlisting the help of these two blundering fools might make it worse tracking the outlaw, but Slocum knew he had no way of getting rid of them short of gunning both down. Trying to explain to the town marshal how the deputy came to get a bullet in the back of his head would give Drury an even greater head start.

"Underwood," Slocum said. He held up his right hand and showed only index finger and thumb.

"He's the one," Harry agreed. He got to his feet, wiped

the blood from his head wound on his coat, and thrust out his hand. "Reckon we're on the same side, after all. Me and Riley took you to be one of the gang."

Slocum shook the bloody hand and resisted the urge to wipe the blood off on his coat.

"We'd better clear out. A dead lawman's going to bring out the whole town."

"This here's a deputy's badge," Riley said, poking the corpse with his rifle barrel. "That must mean a marshal is likely to take offense. You know what we gotta do, Harry."

"We ride. The varmint went that way. You with us, mister?"

Slocum nodded. He was reluctant to let these two hear his name. They'd be caught eventually for murdering the deputy, and the first words out of their mouths would be how John Slocum had put them up to it. He cursed his bad luck when Harry slapped his thigh and declared, "You must be that Slocum gent. Right? That's you? Underwood described you good enough if we ran into each other."

Slocum reluctantly acknowledged, then said, "We're wasting time standing around here."

"Then let's ride!" Riley let out a whoop and headed back toward the restaurant.

Slocum skirted the building and got his horse. The mare looked the better for the quick grooming and some feed and water. Slocum wished he'd had time for the same. What little he had ordered in the restaurant hardly filled him up.

The trio rode past the deputy's body and farther along the trail Drury had taken. Slocum kept a sharp eye out for tracks, but the dirt path carried a considerable amount of both foot and horse traffic, making it impossible to find a single set of boot prints. When the trail curved back downhill, Slocum drew rein and studied the area.

"He kept going, off the path."

"What gives you that idea?" Harry asked.

Slocum had seen a freshly broken twig on a low bush as

well as grass only now popping back up from where a man had trod on it recently. Nothing said this was Drury's doing, but they hadn't come on anyone else following the path, going in either direction.

"There was two of 'em back in the restaurant. That means we kin get rewards for half the gang," Riley said.

"You want to split up and go after the other one?" Harry said. "You think we kin tackle 'em like that, one on one?"

Slocum waited to see what conclusion they reached. Tamara had been absent for so long, he reckoned she had taken up with the gamblers who had been in the game with Drury. But the two specials were right about the man with Drury in the restaurant being another robber. Slocum had overheard enough to know, but if they split and each went after a robber, that left Slocum to decide which man to team up with. Harry and Riley were of a kind, neither a mental giant. That gave Slocum the chance to grab the silver from under the nose of whichever special he took up with.

"We stay with Drury," Riley said, the one of the pair most inclined to worry on such matters.

Slocum felt a little disappointed. Drury was the easy one to nab. The other man wasn't carrying the burden of being a narcotist. Slocum had seen how Drury was suffering from lack of hop. He would make mistakes and even blunder straight for his silver cache with the intent of taking a bar or two into San Francisco and an opium den. Slocum had seen men out of their minds. The drug made them unpredictable, but as long as he kept that in mind, Slocum knew tracking Drury would be easier than the other robber, who had argued against smoking the opium.

"We stick together. That set well with you, Slocum?"

He simply pointed in the direction of the trail he had been following, then urged his mare up a steep slope. Along the rocky trail he saw occasional bright silver streaks where a shod horse had nicked the rock with a sharp-edged steel shoe.

"Dang, Slocum, you could track a ghost through a snow-storm," Harry marveled as they came out along a rise. Even he spotted the trail now. "How'd you learn to follow spoor like that?"

"I bet he was a scout fer the army. You got the look of a man used to bein' out and after Injuns and robbers. That so, Slocum?" Riley looked hard at him.

"You fellows spend most of your time in San Francisco?"

"We don't hit the trail much, if that's what you're sayin'. Harry 'n me, we help out the railroad however we can."

"Collingswood hired you before the robbery?"

"Naw, it's not like that," Harry said. "We do odd jobs, but now and again, Underwood comes up and asks us to do certain chores."

"Union bustin'," Riley said. "They get this bug up their asses that the railroad ought to be closed down. Me and Harry take care of that, but there ain't been so much work like that recently."

Slocum kept his mind on how to find Drury and get away from the two specials. They were strikebreakers and as likely to shoot him in the back once they were done with him as to give him the time of day. Considering how much silver was at stake, Slocum knew they were less likely to return it to the Central California Railroad than they were to keep it for themselves. When they found Drury's cache, splitting it three ways wasn't in the cards either.

"He's headin' there," Harry said in a low voice.

"Shush." His partner sounded like a faulty steam valve as he hissed out the order.

Slocum had overheard the exchange and realized the two specials knew more about Drury's destination than they let on.

"There's a town ahead," Slocum said, staring at a huge plume of rising smoke. "Nobody starts a fire that size without it getting out of control."

The two whispered frantically again. This time he

couldn't overhear but got the gist of what they argued over. Finally Riley rode alongside.

"That there's Newburg. A small mining town that's danged near empty now."

From the smoke, Slocum doubted that. More than one chimney sent that curling plume aloft. They wound around an increasingly well-traveled trail until they came out on a rise looking down on the town. Riley had overstated how much of a ghost town Newburg was. There had to be a couple hundred residents. Slocum cast a sideways look at the two specials. They were whispering furiously again, Riley getting more agitated than his partner.

"We ought to get on down there," Riley said. "That's a good spot to spend the night."

"It's hardly past noon," Slocum said.

"I'm feelin' a mite peaked," Harry piped up. "And it's past mealtime fer me."

Harry might be hungry but it wasn't for food. The smell of silver came from Newburg—or at least the scent of Drury and his partner.

"What was the other one's name?" Slocum asked. "The one with Drury at the restaurant?"

"Heard him called Baldy," said Harry before his partner shushed him.

"Nothing more than that?"

"Harry's likely wrong 'bout that. It might be that Drury knows a lowlife with the moniker of Baldy. That's nothin' to worry over, I'd say."

Slocum rode down the trail toward the town, thinking hard. He had names for all but one of the robbers now. Riley and Harry didn't know about Jackson, and he wasn't inclined to share this with them. Riding with men he didn't trust wasn't all that unusual for Slocum, but seldom did so much money hang in the balance. The two bragged of their employment by the railroad, but this much silver had to tempt a saint. Slocum had given his word to David

Collingswood and would have returned every ounce he found—until the vice president fired him, insulted him, and threw him out.

"I'm feeling a tad dizzy," Slocum said as the two specials passed him to ride on either side. "Why don't you two go on ahead and let me rest here?"

"Partners don't abandon a friend, 'specially a new one. Let's git on over to the saloon and buy you a beer."

Slocum looked around but didn't see a saloon. He rode slowly after the two, who headed to a cross street and took it without a second thought. They had been here before, giving Slocum an uneasy feeling they expected more than Drury to hole up here.

"Ain't much of a saloon, but Newburg ain't much of a town," Harry said, stepping down.

Slocum trailed the other two into the small gin mill but didn't immediately join them at a table toward the rear of the long, narrow room. Windows had been opened at the side of the room to let in some fresh air, but it did little to kill the smell of vomit and spilled, stale beer. Two other customers leaned against the bar, which had once been a thing of beauty. Now too many boot toes had kicked at the front, leaving ugly white gashes, and the surface itself had been scratched deeply. In those wooden trenches, filth and more had accumulated. Slocum tried not to identify the black, gummy substance, but spilled blood came to mind.

"Don't you want some booze, Slocum?" Harry motioned for Slocum to join them.

He walked slowly and studied the two specials. Now that they had reached Newburg, all urgency had passed for finding Drury.

"You been in this town before?"

"Fact is, Slocum, we never knew it existed until we spotted it. But it surely does give a chance for us to kick back and rest 'fore we get on that robber's trail again."

"You don't know if he's in town," Slocum said. "Why not look for him?"

"We need to get some food and maybe swill some of that filthy whiskey you got behind the bar!" Riley spoke loudly enough for the barkeep to grab the bottle and bring over three glasses.

Slocum settled into a chair not already occupied by Riley's boots. The special leaned back, laced his fingers behind his head, and stared up at the ceiling. He let out a long, loud sigh.

"Yes, sir, this is the life. Findin' bad men and drinkin' whiskey." He sat up a bit, took hold of the shot glass, and knocked back the whiskey. He belched loudly, then resumed his position, staring up as if he didn't have a care in the world.

Slocum sipped his shot, made a face, and put it back virtually untouched. He could drink the worst swill, but not this. The trade whiskey had been concocted with too much nitric acid in it. The sip had caused a blister to spring up on his lip. What it would do to his gut had to be a damned sight worse.

"You gonna drink that, Slocum?" Harry pointed to the barely touched drink. When he got a shake of the head, Harry slid it close, then knocked it back. His eyes glazed for a moment, then he sank back and stared out a window.

The change in the two turned Slocum wary. He sat quietly. Silence demanded to be interrupted, and he wanted to hear what they said.

"You know, Slocum, this is the kind of place where we ought to rest up. Me and Harry are about at the end of our rope."

"You'd let me keep on after Drury?"

"You're more dedicated than me and Harry," Riley said. "Mr. Collingswood made a durned good decision hirin' you on."

"I'm going to look around town, ask some questions."

"You do that," Harry said. "Me and Riley, we ain't got enough energy to budge. You can find us here when you get tired of nosin' around."

They signaled for another drink. Slocum pushed away from the table and left the saloon, his mind racing. They had wanted his tracking skills, but once they caught sight of the town, they wanted to get rid of him. That meant they knew something they hadn't shared. Slocum decided they had overheard Drury and his partner say something, maybe about meeting in a town when they split up. This was the town.

He walked slowly up one side of the main street and down the other, looking inside every store for any trace of the outlaws. More than once, he asked after Drury and his partner, Baldy. No one had seen them—or nobody fessed up to it. Slocum was good at reading a bluff across a poker table and almost as good at seeing when he was being handed a line. The good citizens of Newburg weren't lying. The ones he had asked hadn't seen the train robbers.

After an hour of reconnaissance, he returned to the saloon, where Harry and Riley still sat at the back table. They huddled together, whispering. Neither saw him and neither showed any inclination to budge from their chair. For two men inclined to shoot first and aim later, they showed a great deal of patience.

They were waiting for Drury and Baldy.

Slocum went to the livery stable and let the stableboy tend to his trusty mare. For a railroad horse, the animal had been remarkably dependable, and Slocum wanted to show his appreciation. There had to be more hard riding ahead, and he wanted to be ready.

Slocum settled into a chair on the boardwalk across the street from the livery stable and continued to evaluate his options. When he finally got up, he walked briskly to the telegraph office. The telegrapher looked up from a week-old *Alta California*.

"I need to send a couple telegrams."

"That's why I'm here. Send enough and you can make my week."

"Been slow?" Slocum watched the young man closely. The telegrapher twirled the tips of his thin handlebar mustache. He was old enough to grow some facial hair but young enough that it had to be a chore. That made him even prouder to show it off. Slocum saw no reason not to build the boy's confidence with a compliment about the mustache.

"Thank you kindly. Every man in the family's growed a big one. You shoulda seen my granddday's. I do declare, it went out to here." Like a man lying about how big the fish he'd caught, he held his hands on either side of his head.

"A regular longhorn, your grandpa," Slocum said. He took a blank pad of telegraph forms and wrote swiftly.

"Time for me to get to work," the young man said, obviously disappointed that he didn't get to brag more. He took the telegram and looked at it. "You said you had more 'n one to send."

"I want that sent to the Central California Railroad depot in Oakland, to the main office in San Francisco, and to the postmaster in the next town over."

"Next town? You mean Fremont?"

"I do."

The telegrapher scratched his head, then looked up at Slocum. "This is mighty strange. Don't you know where this T. Crittenden is?"

"Not exactly, but one of those people'll know where to deliver the message."

"Your money. Ain't never seen anything like this before since 'grams are so expensive, but you're sendin' it to railroad men, so—"

"I'm charging it to the Central California Railroad." Slocum took out the papers he'd received from Collingswood and laid them on the counter. "This is my authority."

"Send 'em and collect from the railroad?"

Slocum saw the calculation working in the young man's eyes.

"I'm trusting you to send an honest bill, but Mr. Collingswood has to know how difficult this is for you and will pay accordingly."

"He's the vice president, all right. I applied for a job, and I seen him. Not personally, mind you, but he was talkin' to the foreman doin' the hirin'."

"I can't imagine how he let a crackerjack telegrapher go unhired."

Slocum took back his sheaf of papers and tucked them away. They had come in handy again. If Collingswood refused to pay, Slocum would be long gone when the bill was brought to his attention.

And with any luck, Tamara would have received a telegram telling her to come to Newburg.

11

"Two days," Slocum said. "I thought you'd be here quicker."

Tamara Crittenden laughed, and it was the sound of morning bells and soft evening breezes slipping through the pines. She reached over and put her warm hand on Slocum's arm, squeezing gently.

"I came as fast as I could. The stationmaster in Oakland gave me the message. It was such a surprise."

"You didn't think I'd get in touch with you?"

Slocum sat stolidly as she squeezed down just a little harder, then moved her hand away. They both looked up as the waiter brought them their breakfast. The runny eggs and leathery steaks gave off an unappetizing odor, but Slocum dug into his. It had been too long since he'd eaten. Since sending the telegrams, he had hardly left the saloon and the other two specials. Harry and Riley had gotten knee-walking drunk on the cheap trade whiskey, and he doubted they could have won a fight with a newborn kitten if the need had arisen. While he saw they were lacking in intelligence, both had a cunning that told him they'd not risk their own hides needlessly. They were waiting and knew the train robbers wouldn't show up while they were drunk on their asses.

"Oh, I never doubted you would. I meant that the lazy stationmaster showed some initiative in tracking me down. It was a good thing I asked after the two gamblers from Fremont, or he might not have known I was even in town."

"Why did you follow them?"

"I didn't know if they were involved in the robbery. Besides, you had Drury dead to rights." She reached out and brushed away a lock of greasy hair from his eyes. "You were roughed up, weren't you?"

"The barkeep tried to drug me, but it didn't work out so well for him."

"Not if he thought you were any kind of victim." Tamara sat back in her chair, eyed the breakfast with distaste, then began sawing at the steak. She held up the piece she'd cut off and stared at it. "If I needed my boot sole patched, this would work." She stuffed it into her mouth and began chewing. "My boots would have better flavor."

Slocum grunted as he worked on his own meal.

"Why do you think they aren't budging?" Tamara asked.

"They overheard Drury and Baldy say something about this town."

"Baldy? He's another one? We know Jack, Drury, and now Baldy. There were four." Tamara dropped her fork onto the plate with a loud clang. She sipped at the coffee, made a face, and kept drinking.

"I haven't told them that Jackson's dead."

"That's smart. Never show your hand until the pot's called."

Slocum looked at her. A tiny smile curled her lips. She was joshing him, and he found that he liked it.

"They haven't seen you. You might get them to reveal something that I'd have to beat out of them."

"From the sound of those two, beating it out of them would be more enjoyable." She delicately dabbed her lips and then used the napkin to clean off the rim of the coffee cup. Another quick sip. She made a face. "The dirt made it almost drinkable."

"The lousy chow's the reason Newburg is turning into a ghost town. Do you think the robbers rendezvoused here because of that?"

"Why don't I see what our two erstwhile railroad specials have to say while you ask after Drury and Baldy?"

"I've not heard anyone talk about strangers, other than me, Harry, and Riley." He grinned. "With you in town, there's going to be plenty of tongues set to wagging."

"Why, Mr. Slocum, is that a compliment?" She lowered her voice and locked eyes with him. "Or is it a promise to do something to me that will positively outrage these fine, upstanding townspeople into salacious gossip?"

"Not to you, with you," he said, pushing back his chair and standing. He drew hers back. She pressed briefly against him, giving her hip just the right amount of touch against his groin to cement the promise of doing something outrageous later.

She left without so much as a backward look at him, but he watched as she went down the street to the saloon. The hitch in her git-along was as promising as her words. He dropped a greenback dollar on the table and went outside to start asking after the robbers. He came down the far side of the street and saw that Tamara had lured Riley and Harry from the saloon and out onto the splintered boardwalk. She crowded both men, and they reacted with what Slocum had come to believe was common among wranglers. The attention of such a lovely woman thrilled them as much as it frightened them. Riley tried to brag. His words echoed across the street, but Harry hung back, licking his lips and waiting for his chance to swoop in should Tamara reject his partner.

When she did, Harry stepped up, but Riley caught his arm. For a moment Slocum thought they'd come to blows. Then Harry swung his partner around. Both men stared down the street. When they went for their six-shooters, Slocum turned to see what interested them more than Tamara.

He cursed under his breath. Drury and Baldy rode in from the north. Drury had seen better days. Always thin, he looked as if he had one foot in the grave now. His face was paper white and his eyes burned with balefire. In spite of his condition, he spotted the specials before Baldy.

Harry and Riley went for their guns, but Drury got off the first shot. No matter that he looked like death warmed over, he proved more accurate than either of the specials, too. Harry yelped as hot lead tore past his cheek. A spatter of blood caused him to wipe furiously to clear his right eye so he could sight. As he rubbed, Riley got his smoke wagon firing, but his accuracy was less than adequate for the task. His rounds all went wide, giving Drury and Baldy the chance to wheel about and gallop away.

Slocum moved into the street, his Colt leveled, but the chance to join the fight had passed.

"You stepped in front of me, John." Tamara's voice was choked.

"Did you get hit?"

"You blocked them from hitting me. That's why you weren't able to gun them down."

Slocum had instinctively put himself between the woman and the outlaws. This had prevented him from getting a good shot.

"Those two fools scared them off. Now we'll have to chase them down."

"My horse is in the stable, in the stall next to yours."

"Come on." Slocum took Tamara's elbow and hurried her along to the livery, where the stableboy stood in the middle of the street, his mouth gaping.

"Did you see that? Them two gents started firing, and the two on horseback shot back and—"

"We need our mounts," Slocum said, shaking the boy out of his shock. "Now."

"I'll get them for you."

He vanished into the stable. Slocum started to speak but

found himself saving Tamara again, this time from a
wagon clattering down the street at a breakneck speed. His
arm snaked around her trim waist, and he spun her about
out of the way of the rig. For a brief instant, he reached for
his gun, but then relaxed. Taking a shot at the reckless driver
accomplished nothing. He had probably been spooked like
the rest of the sleepy town. With a declining population,
those most inclined to shoot it out had left for more spirited
towns.

"Thanks again," Tamara said, catching her breath and
patting her hair back into place. "That's twice in a couple
minutes that you've saved me."

"The driver was in a powerful hurry to get out of town."
Slocum stared after the empty wagon.

"Here's your horses," said the stableboy, handing over
the reins.

"You know who that was in the wagon?"

"Ain't seen him before. He bought the wagon from Old
Man Hansen. You know him. The fellow who wears that
leather mask. Got his face all blowed up in a mine explo-
sion. Tore the skin right off down to the bone, or so they
say. He wears it so he won't scare the kids." The stableboy
coughed and looked sheepish. "Truth is, he'd scare me out
of my wits if his face is half as ugly as everyone claims."

"The wagon driver," Slocum said. "You don't know him?"

"That's what I said. You hard of hearin,' mister? Old Man
Hansen's sorta deaf, too. Blowed an ear off and—"

Slocum swung into the saddle. Tamara stepped up onto
her horse and rode close.

"What's wrong, John?"

"Nothing," he said, seeing that the wagon had vanished
down the road leading due west.

He put his heels to the mare's flanks and trotted off,
Tamara keeping pace. Staring in the direction taken by
Drury and Baldy, Slocum turned cold. The two specials had
gotten to their horses but found it difficult getting mounted.

Both men sported wounds from the brief gunfight, Harry having taken the worst of it.

"Hey, wait!" Riley shouted. His foot tangled in the stirrup, and his horse started, forcing him to hop along. "Slocum, you can't go after 'em. Them's our outlaws to arrest."

"They know I'm with you now," Tamara said.

"Did you learn anything at all from them?"

"Not much more than what you'd guessed. They overheard Drury and Baldy talking about coming here. Even those dimwits understood what that meant."

"Where would they stash the stolen silver?" Slocum was thinking aloud and didn't expect an answer. He tried to visualize the lay of the land.

They were some distance from the railroad tracks and much farther from where the train had been robbed on the steep grade leading to the pass.

"This is the town closest to the robbery, John," Tamara said. "Are you still here or has your mind wandered off like a little lost sheep?"

"Sorry," Slocum said. He kept trying to understand what was going on.

All the two specials cared about was getting the drop on the outlaws or maybe gunning them down so they could take scalps in for the reward. Slocum knew he had to be smarter than that. Collingswood had hired him to bring in the outlaws, then fired him. Retrieving the silver was going to make for a fine payday, but Slocum knew a quarter of it was already lost when Jackson died.

"Off the road," Slocum said suddenly. He trotted into a ditch and followed the channel uphill to a stand of trees.

"There they are," Tamara said with some distaste as Harry and Riley galloped past.

"There's no way we can find the outlaws. Drury was too spooked. He and Baldy would split up and get together somewhere else."

"You can find them, though, can't you, John?"

He shook his head. The outlaws had enough head start to lay a trap. Any ambush would get rid of the two specials, but Slocum thought Drury and Baldy wouldn't stay together. Once they split up, they doubled their chances of outrunning pursuit. The land around was forested and hilly, making tracking difficult. He might get lucky and find a trace, but Slocum doubted it. So far his luck had been poor.

Standing around Newburg for two days waiting for the outlaws—and Tamara—to arrive had made him antsy. Harry and Riley presented as much a danger to him as the train robbers.

"We can't let them ride away," Tamara protested. "Think, John, where would they go? You're the expert. Where would an outlaw hide?"

"They want to take the silver and hightail it. The three remaining outlaws intend to load it on a wagon and get away from here. With the railroad sending out posses, the outlaws' anxiety over losing the silver has to be great. Their own lives would be forfeit if they were caught, but with so many riders scouring the countryside, the silver is at risk of being found."

"How does that get us on to Drury and Baldy's trail?"

"Back to town."

"Town, but—" Tamara stared at him. Then her eyes widened and she smiled. "The wagon that almost ran us over. You think that was the third robber?"

"We won't find the other two, not with Harry and Riley on their trail."

"You're so clever. You asked the stable hand if the driver was a local."

"He had never seen the man before. That doesn't make him a robber, but the coincidence is too much to ignore."

She bent over so her lips brushed his cheek.

"You're a genius, and I love you! Come on. Time's wasting!"

They made their way back to Newburg and immediately took the same road as the reckless wagon driver.

"Did you get a good look at him, John?" Tamara glanced in his direction as they rode almost knee to knee. "I heard the horses and the wagon, but you swept me off my feet too fast to see him."

"I didn't," Slocum said, distracted by her nearness and trying to work out which of the wagon tracks belonged to the driver whom he felt in his gut to be the last of the gang. "I can't find the tracks, so we need to ride fast."

"Fast? I like it hard," she said, giving him a broad wink.

Slocum put his heels to the mare and rocketed away. Tamara kept up, but her horse flagged before Slocum's, forcing him to slow and finally to come to a halt. He didn't understand what was wrong. They had topped more than one rise in the steep road and had a view miles ahead. No one was on the road, much less the wagon and its driver.

"We can't keep going like this," she said, patting her horse's neck.

"Walk the horse, trot, then gallop, walk, change the gait, and rest a few minutes."

"That'll cover a lot of distance, but why haven't we overtaken the wagon by now? We've ridden for more than an hour and covered more distance than he ever could have."

Slocum nodded agreement. He had thought the same thing. They hadn't been more than an hour behind the departing wagon and traveled twice as fast—or more.

"We keep going another half hour, then we decide what to do."

"I need to rest. So does my horse."

"We can rest in a half hour. Change gait, cover ground." He led off. Tamara gamely followed, but he soon saw that her mount stumbled and would soon collapse under her.

At the end of the half hour, they had covered another three miles without sighting the wagon. Slocum hadn't noticed anywhere the driver had left the road, and it was inconceivable they hadn't overtaken the rig by now.

He voiced his concern.

"He might have tried running us over, gone a ways out of town, then circled around," suggested Tamara. "That means we'd have to choose another road and—"

"He didn't," Slocum said positively. "We would have seen him if he'd gone after Drury and Baldy. The road south is too steep and goes away from the silver, wherever it's hidden." He pointed ahead. "East along this road takes us to a spot near the train robbery—"

"Where the silver is hidden," she finished. With a sharp intake of breath and a release that set her breasts to shaking delightfully, she said, "What can we do?"

"Rest the horses, set up camp here, where we can see the road but not be seen."

Tamara smiled. "I understand. If we missed the wagon between here and town, if he had hidden somewhere along the road, he'll have to pass us to get to the silver cache."

"I can use some grub."

"And a rest," Tamara said, but Slocum heard the contradiction in her voice.

He dismounted and led his mare to a spot that gave a good view of the road through the trees. The driver would be almost on them before he noticed anyone watching, while Slocum had a view giving more than fifteen minutes' warning of any traveler. He gathered wood and made a small fire while Tamara prepared the food for cooking. They worked in silence, exchanged only a few words while they ate, then spread out their blankets and lay back.

But it wasn't to rest.

The tension had been growing between them all day—since Slocum had rescued her from getting run over.

"I want to thank you," Tamara said.

"The wagon?"

"No, for this." She pressed her hand down on his crotch. He had been hard for some time.

"If you like it, why don't you take it out?"

Her fingers danced over the buttons and popped the fly open. His manhood rushed out, tall and proud and straining.

"I'm afraid you might be chilly, all naked and hanging out like that."

Before he could say a word, she dropped down and enmouthed his length. He gasped as her tongue swirled about the sensitive tip and then worked down the underside to poke into his balls. She kept pressing and pulling until she had him fully out of his jeans and could concentrate her full oral assault on him. Sucking hard on the plum-sized tip, her cheeks went hollow, and Slocum thought he would go crazy with lust.

His hips lifted from the blanket as he tried to sink deeper into her mouth. She held her head stationary and let him thrust until he bounced off the roof of her mouth and went deeper into her throat. When she swallowed, he felt the motion all around his hidden length. It sent a shockwave along his fleshy shaft and into his loins. He knew what a forest felt like now as a fire crept closer and eventually engulfed it. Slow heat, warmer, hotter, fierce heat that devoured body and soul. Her fingers stroked over his hairy balls and then tugged. Slocum had to concentrate not to lose control. Everything she did with her mouth, how she fondled him, the heat of her gusting breath against his groin, all conspired to push his arousal up more and more.

She began bobbing her head up and down, mimicking the motion that suddenly appealed more to him than having her lips stroking the sides of his erection.

He reached down and pushed her away.

"Your turn," he said. Her bright eyes turned into small suns, burning with lust.

She went end for end and straddled his head, her knees beside his ears.

"No, I want—"

"Lick," she ordered. "All over. I want to feel your tongue on my body like this."

She bent down and sucked him into her mouth again. Slocum groaned and sank back. Looking up, all he saw was a mountain of cloth. He began pushing away her skirts until he exposed her legs. Caressing her thighs brought immediate response. She sucked harder. He ran his hands along the insides of her legs, letting the sleek flesh flow like satin under his fingertips. When he succeeded in getting her skirts bunched around her hips, he saw the delicious target she wanted him to sample.

He reared up and applied his mouth to her privates. In reaction, she worked even more furiously on his manhood. He kissed her nether lips, then ran his tongue along the pinkly scalloped flaps until they trembled. Tasting the thick juices oozing from her interior spurred him on. Grabbing her around the legs, he pulled her hips down so she spread wider across his face.

His tongue shot out and ran about, just within the portal to her heated center. She trembled as he continued to explore orally. At the same time he knew his own genitals were getting full attention from her mouth. He pulled her down more so he could drive his tongue deeper into her. Then he raced around the rim of her opening.

Tamara emitted small sounds of passion, without once releasing her lips from their station over the end of his cock. Then she started bobbing up and down, taking him faster and faster. He matched her pace until she began grinding her hips into his face in obvious, silent demand for what she wanted most. He thrust in and out with his tongue and then his world exploded. Tension mounted and he found himself unable to restrain the white-hot rush. He spewed forth his load, and she sucked it all up as she squeezed down hard on his balls.

The rush of sensation passed, and he renewed his tonguing until her legs clamped down hard on either side of his head and she shook hard as if caught in an earthquake. Then she stretched out, her legs straight on either side of his head.

Slocum disengaged, rolled over, and came up to lie with her in his arms.

"That was incredible, John. And you taste so good!"

He kissed her almost as hard as she kissed back. Before the sun sank behind the mountains to the west, they found new ways of enjoying each other.

And the wagon never passed them.

12

"How can this be, John?" Tamara Crittenden stood in the middle of Newburg's main street, staring at the deserted buildings in disbelief. One or two curious residents still in the town poked their heads out, looked at her, then went back to their business, meager though it was.

Slocum turned in a complete circle and shook his head.

"He gave us the slip. I'm damned if I know how he did it. If he'd hidden the wagon along that road and ridden on horseback from there, he'd have had to pass us."

"He didn't. And there weren't any side roads."

"Not that I saw." He took a deep breath and let it out slowly. They had ridden back to town and had spent the last hour asking anyone who would talk to them if they had seen the driver and his wagon.

The answer to both had been a puzzled "no." More than one curious citizen asked why they were interested. From the responses, Slocum doubted the train robber had bought off everyone. After asking the same question so many times, one of the men interrogated would have shown a hint of lying. All were honestly mystified. Newburg wasn't a town where anyone got lost. It was too tiny and getting smaller by the day as the last of the diehards moved on to greener pastures.

"You looked? Hard?"

He turned on her. The flash of anger silenced the woman. Slocum took it as an insult to his talent and his integrity that he had missed the trick that had allowed a man driving a wagon to simply vanish.

"I'm sorry. I hunted for tracks, too, and I saw nothing leading away from the road. Even identifying the ones made when he left town after nearly running me down didn't amount to a hill of beans."

"The wagon tracks disappeared in the dust before the first hill," Slocum said. He'd gone over every possible tactic and come up with nothing. "Abandoning the wagon and riding the team away is all I can figure."

"Then he'll have to get another wagon if he wants to load the silver and drive off with it," she said.

Slocum walked to a spot in the shade and sat on the edge of the uneven boardwalk. The rough plank under him reminded him of the times he had been whipped for misbehaving when he was a young boy in school. He hadn't been the best student and had paid for his sass. Now he thought of the splintery boards against his ass as new punishment for not being good enough. Pushing his failure from his mind, he went back over everything he had learned about the robbery. The three had come to this town and had fled when the two specials opened fire on them instead of trapping them good and proper.

Where Riley and Harry had gone was anyone's guess. After Baldy and Drury made the most sense. That left the remaining robber running around loose without anyone in pursuit because Slocum had screwed up and—

He stood abruptly.

"Mount up. We're riding to the place where the train was robbed."

"Waiting there won't get us anywhere," Tamara said. "Wherever Jack hid his share, it was quite a ways off from the tracks."

"It's the only place all the robbers have in common. If they split up, we can avoid following Jackson's trail since it didn't bring us to where he hid the silver. That improves our chances of finding not only the other three's trails but also their caches."

"I suppose. Jack was always a suspicious sort, sure everyone wanted to double-cross him."

Slocum said nothing. The outlaw's instincts had been accurate when it came to Tamara. Avoiding his partners had been a smart move, too. But were the remaining three more trusting of one another? The wagon suggested they were, unless each of their cuts from the robbery required a wagon to cart off. That sent him thinking along other roads, only to be nudged from his reverie when Tamara shook his shoulder.

"You got all distant, John. What are you thinking?"

"The place where they robbed the train. It's all we have."

"I suppose so," she said reluctantly. "Let's get supplies for the trail." She hesitated, then asked, "Should we get a pack animal or two? For when we find the silver?"

"We'll worry about moving it after we find it," he said. Slocum considered how many silver bars he could load into his saddlebags and how far he could ride his old mare weighed down like that.

"We can always hide it in a different spot," she said. Her eyes sparkled with greed. "That's if we don't shoot them all down. If we did, there wouldn't be any reason to move the silver. Just take what we could and return for the rest when we liked."

"Don't count your chickens before they're hatched. That's what my grandma always told me, and it's good advice."

"You're always so glum, John. Live a little. Think of all the wonderful things you could do with a mountain of silver.

Think of what *we* could do, the places to go. I've always wanted to see Paris and London, dress in fine European gowns, and attend fancy balls thrown by the aristocracy. We would make such a splash! The crowned heads of Europe would bow to us, the fabulously wealthy Americans."

Slocum knew it was more likely that they would be, even if the silver rose up in a huge mound before them, spurned as uncouth barbarians. He had ridden with enough Europeans to get sick of their superior airs. One had been a remittance man, the third son of a British lord depending on his pa's largesse every month, and he had been insufferable in spite of being a leech and totally dependent on a man across the Atlantic who paid to keep him away. More than once the remittance man had drunk up his allowance by the middle of the month and begged for pennies to get more whiskey. The last Slocum had seen of him was his back as he rode away in Montana, sure that one day his older brothers would die and he would inherit the family estates. As drunk as he had been, Slocum wondered if he might not realize that dream.

More than once, the remittance man had been as drunk as a lord. All he needed was the title to go with tying on the bender.

"Everyone needs a dream," he told Tamara. "I've always wanted to own an Appaloosa stud farm up in Oregon, but the trail never led that way." She looked at him strangely, then stepped up into the saddle, settled herself, and waited for him to mount.

They rode from town on the trail of the stolen silver.

"This is the place," Tamara said, walking up the railroad tracks. The steep grade made her a tad breathless.

Slocum enjoyed the sight of her breasts rising and falling with the exertion. He felt a little lack of air, too, but not as much. They had tired their horses so much they had to let them rest for the remainder of the day. But they had found the stretch of track where the robbery had occurred. He ignored her and worked out how the four thieves had rushed the mail car.

He looked down the steep embankment and shuddered. Falling from the side of the mountain would be a messy death. He put his back to the sheer drop and pretended the mail car had halted just in front of him. The robbers would rush forward, their six-shooters blazing. The mail clerk wouldn't be able to fight them off—and then the four robbers would stand in the car, stunned by their good luck. What they had thought to be a few hundred dollars had become ten thousand in heavy silver bars. Maybe more. Tamara didn't know the exact amount, and Collingswood never revealed it.

The vice president had to be stewing in his own juices by now. To report such a loss to the president and board of directors would get him fired immediately. If he was lucky, he'd only be fired. If the men running the Central California Railroad were like most of the businessmen in San Francisco, David Collingswood could count himself lucky if he didn't find himself in the crew of a China clipper bound for the Flowery Kingdom. Three years at sea hardly recovered the silver but the board of directors, if they were the least bit law-abiding, wouldn't slit his throat and dump him into the Bay.

Shanghaiing him was a better punishment all around.

"They uncoupled the cars and they rolled back downhill," Slocum said, more to himself than to Tamara.

He paid no attention to where she went, being lost in reliving the robbery. The weight of the silver had made applying the mail car's brake more difficult. The caboose had derailed. He found the bright silver nicks in the steel track where the car had tumbled over, away from the cliff. Farther downhill he found the spot where the brake had finally brought the mail car to a halt. From the damage to the tracks, the car had slid off the rails here but remained upright.

Repair crews had worked to erase the worst of the damage, but Slocum knew riding along this stretch of track, even at the slow speed necessary when going uphill, would be rough. A shudder when he thought of highballing downhill coming from the coast over this damaged section told him how much he preferred riding. Even the old mare under him was safer than hitting this stretch at high speed and going over the brink to the canyon floor so far below because of a defective rail.

All traces of the mail car and caboose had been removed. He imagined crews loading the pieces into freight cars or onto flat bed cars. Or had the Central California Railroad crew levered both back onto the tracks and let another engine pull them to a dcpot? He hadn't bothered to ask since the actual cars, if they had been put onto a siding, gave him no useful information. Walking back along the tracks, he tried to find any trace of Jackson and the others' horses as they carried away the hundreds of silver bars. Too much time had passed. Any chance of tracking here had gone with wind and rain and the passage of dozens of other trains, not to mention the repair crews.

He knelt, ran his fingers over the cool steel rail, then looked up into a blinding reflection from a low hill on the far side of the tracks. Not consciously thinking, Slocum twisted violently and threw himself flat on the ground. Cinders cut into his chest, and he scraped his cheek against a metal burr on the track. The discomfort from these minor scrapes was nothing compared to having his head blown off.

The bullet sailed just above him and out over the canyon.

He wiggled fast like a sidewinder and slid over the verge. His feet found a rocky ledge for support. Peering over the edge, he caught sight of the reflection again. The sniper was too far away for him to use his Colt. Still, the temptation to draw and send some of the six-gun's slugs in that direction almost overcame common sense.

"John, John!"

"Stay down," he bellowed. "Take cover. There's a gun-man on a hill a hundred yards away."

He ducked as a rifle bullet tore past his head.

"What are we going to do? He can keep us pinned down here forever."

"Or until another train comes along," Slocum said. He had no idea when that would be. The ledge where he stood was too shallow for him to sit and wait out the sniper. "Can you draw his fire without getting shot?"

"I don't know. I think I can. What are you going to do?"

Slocum gathered his strength, found a hole in the rock for his toe, then waited. Tamara moved fifty feet uphill from him, drawing attention away. When the sniper fired on her, Slocum reacted. He kicked hard and launched himself back to the level railroad bed. This time he didn't use the tracks as a partial shelter. He ran for all he was worth in a frontal assault on the rifleman.

It took only a split second for the gunman to realize Slocum was turning the tables and get off another shot. Dodging, moving fast, Slocum presented a poor target. He saw a couple more bullets kick up dirt around him. One lead slug spanged off a rail. In spite of the death around him in the air, Slocum made his way to the foot of the hill where the sniper fired.

Now he whipped out his six-shooter and squeezed off a couple rounds at what he thought was an exposed elbow. Curses came his way but not from winging his foe. At best he had caused him to move. A few more rounds came Slo-cum's way, but the sniper no longer had a clear shot. Using scrubby trees for cover, Slocum inched up the slope until he got to the top of the hill. The spent brass glittered in the afternoon sun, but the rocky stretch gave no hint as to the direction the gunman had taken in his retreat.

Slocum closed his eyes for a moment and used other senses. A faint whiff of tobacco lingered. The gunman had recently smoked a cigar. But distant sounds of bushes snap-ping back as a man pushed through them caused Slocum to turn in that direction before opening his eyes. The gunman wasn't anywhere to be seen, but faint sounds of his passage through the underbrush sent Slocum in that direction at a dead run.

When he got to the bushes where the sniper had fled, he found broken twigs and freshly crushed leaves on the ground. He hunted for his quarry, but the man had disappeared into thin air. Listening again, Slocum tried to locate the gunman but couldn't. Either he had realized how he was being tracked and had gone to ground or he had already escaped.

Advancing more cautiously now, Slocum followed the path. An angry bull might have plowed through the vegetation. Trailing the gunman was easy. Slocum quickly realized the man was circling the hill, heading back toward the tracks.

"Damnation," he said under his breath.

Leaving Tamara by herself might have been a fatal mistake. The sniper circled around to get the drop on her. Slocum estimated distances, then ran back up the hill since this was the fastest path to the tracks. Atop the hill, he looked down but saw nothing of the woman. Like the bull he had imagined charging through the brush, he roared downhill and came out on the tracks. He looked up along the tracks and didn't see her. Then he heard the metallic click of a shell being levered into a rifle's chamber.

He dropped flat as a bullet tore past. Again he used the tracks for shelter, but this time the gunman was back down the tracks, able to shoot parallel to the rails.

Slocum rolled onto his back and got off a couple rounds. Then he raised his hands, his gun still clutched in his right hand. He stared down the barrel leveled at him from ten feet away.

"Drop the hogleg," the man said.

"You were in Newburg," Slocum said, playing for time. "You drove the wagon that damned near ran over me."

"Too bad I missed. Drop the gun." The man snugged the rifle stock to his shoulder.

Slocum did as he was told, though he knew it was likely the last thing he would do. The man's knuckle turned white as he squeezed down on the rifle trigger.

13

Slocum saw death in the man's burning eyes. He started to grab for his six-gun when the outlaw fired. To his surprise, Slocum didn't feel the hot streak of lead ripping through his body. The bullet sailed past his head and whined away into the distance. With a quick jerk, he brought his six-shooter up and trained it on his attacker, only to find himself pointing the muzzle at Tamara Crittenden.

She smiled as she tossed a rock the size of her fist to the ground.

"You can thank me," she said. "If I'd been a second later, he would have killed you."

Slocum stared at the man on the ground, moaning and reaching for the bloody patch on the back of his head where Tamara had clipped him. Before the outlaw could recover, Slocum plucked the rifle from the man's nerveless fingers and let him use both hands to hold his head. Blood oozed down and soaked his filthy coat collar.

"This is the same man who drove the wagon," Slocum said. He prodded the felled man with the toe of his boot. "How did you hide the wagon?"

"John, please. Is that important now?"

It was to Slocum. He prided himself on his tracking abilities, and this train robber had successfully thrown him off the trail. Finding out how let him learn how to avoid such a mistake in the future—or gave him reason to appreciate how dangerous the man could be. Being outsmarted rankled.

"The wagon," he repeated.

"Where did you hide your share of the stolen silver?" Tamara pushed Slocum aside to ask her question. "We can make a deal for it."

"Like hell we will," Slocum said, his anger rising.

The outlaw looked up at them, confused. He tried to shake his head, but the pain forced him to stop.

"You work for the railroad?" he grated out.

Slocum and Tamara exchanged a quick look, then both answered that they did. Slocum went further and pulled the sheaf of papers Collingswood had given him as proof of his position as a special detective.

"I can't read," the man said.

"You're lying," Slocum said. He saw the way the man's eyes had scanned the page, stopped at the bottom, and then worked back over details of what legal authority had been granted. The outlaw understood well enough what Slocum had been empowered to do. He just didn't know that Slocum had been fired or Tamara had walked away from her job as the vice president's assistant.

"You trailed me. I thought you were road agents. How was I to know you're railroad dicks?" He looked from Slocum to Tamara. His eyes lingered on her form, the tears in her clothing revealing tantalizing glimpses of bare skin. "Got to say, I never saw a railroad detective who looked like you."

"Remember who crowned you with a rock," Tamara said hotly. "I can do it again. Or maybe I'll take a short walk and leave you in the custody of the man you were going to murder."

Slocum lifted his pistol and pointed it between the man's eyes.

"What's your name?"

"Montague. I'm just riding back to San Francisco. You don't have anything on me."

"Pierre Montague?" Tamara stared at him. "Yes, you're Pierre Montague."

"What if I am?"

"The Central California Railroad has a standing warrant out for your arrest. You steal company property from our depots."

"That's not me," Montague said, turning surly. He winced as he probed the wound on his skull.

Slocum pulled Tamara back a few paces so they could discuss their prisoner without being overheard. He kept his Colt Navy trained on the outlaw and never looked at Tamara as they spoke.

"Did the railroad have a wanted poster out for him, or did Jackson tell you the names of his gang?"

"Oh, John, I've told you. Jack was the only one I knew. He kept all the details of the robbery and his gang close to the vest. Montague *does* have an alert out on him. He's stolen a considerable amount of freight from the Oakland yard and is suspected of petty theft in both Sacramento and Virginia City." She saw his skeptical look. "I saw the warrant when it was on Mr. Collingswood's desk. I can be a very snoopy person when I put my mind to it."

"That's how you found out about the silver shipment," Slocum said.

"Yes, and it's how I found out about you." She moved closer, but Slocum stepped back. Tamara started to protest, but Slocum silenced her.

"Montague won't talk. I've seen his kind before, and he will die before he tells us where the silver is hidden."

"He and the other two have formed their own gang. They must have left all their shares from the robbery in a single place." Tamara hardly contained her excitement at this. Slocum had to dissuade her.

"We don't know that. I think Jackson going his own way tells the story. They didn't trust each other. We can play on that distrust."

"You mean I can play on it, don't you, John?" Tamara grinned. "You saw how he stared at me. It's the same way you do when you think I'm not looking."

Slocum couldn't disagree with her. He grew impatient with the endless futile search for the stolen silver. Riley and Harry were greedy and hunting for the same treasure trove. David Collingswood might have sent out an army of other railroad dicks on the same mission.

"Go on," he said softly. Louder, "You're loco. We have to get rid of him before the train comes."

"There is a reward on his head."

"It's nothing compared to the reward for finding the silver." Slocum saw her face light up as she understood what to say.

"We did a good job on that, John. Mr. Collingswood will give us a bigger reward for getting so much back. Although the reward for Montague is only a few dollars, it's more than we have now."

"We let the crew load the silver. There's no need to get greedy when we've done our job."

"And you've done it so well, John." She ran her hand down his chest. Her fingers danced lightly and slipped under his vest to press into his gently beating heart. "Are you sure we can't, umm, sample some of the silver before they take it back to San Francisco?"

"No. That'd be stealing, just like that son of a bitch and his partners did. The silver belongs to the railroad."

"You're right, of course." She stepped away and cast a quick look at Montague, who took in every word they said. "Is that the train coming now?"

"I can't tell."

"Go up to the summit and look. I'll guard our prisoner."

Slocum nodded, whispered, "Be careful," and then rushed off without a backward look.

He went a dozen paces and stopped, pretending to wait for a train highballing from Oakland.

Tamara's steps crunched on cinders as she went back to Montague. She made no effort to keep her voice low.

"He doesn't know that it'll take a week before the train arrives to recover the silver. Can you get away with it all before then?"

"What silver?" Montague said suspiciously.

"I'm tired of him. He wants to return all the silver to the railroad. They don't need it. The Central California Railroad is filthy rich—like I want to be. You and me, we can team up."

Montague surged, but Tamara had her .22-caliber pistol out and trained on him.

"Neither of us gets rich if you don't throw in with me," she said. "You will be hanged or spend a very long time in prison. San Quentin always has another cell waiting for a train robber."

"You'd double-cross him?"

"We found the silver, but there's so much of it. You have the wagon you bought back in Newburg?"

"I hid it and rode the team. With two horses, we can get a lot of the silver from the hiding place."

"I just have my horse. You've got both from the team?"

"I'm riding one. The other can be used as a pack animal."

"How far do you think we can get in a week? I don't know these things."

"Far enough that they'll never catch us," Montague said. "You've got the gun. Kill him, and we'll get the silver."

"I can trust you?"

"You were the one who told Jackson about the shipment, weren't you? So you're already on the wrong side of the law."

Tamara laughed.

"I wondered how long it would take for you to figure that

out. He doesn't know." She jerked her thumb in Slocum's direction.

"Shoot him, and we can get on the way. To the silver."

Tamara turned and started walking toward Slocum. He watched her and tried not to smile as she lifted her Colt New Line and pointed it in his direction. From where Montague stood, it had to look as if she had him dead in her sights. When she fired, Slocum threw himself backward and flopped onto his back. She had fired a couple feet to his left.

She came over and looked down at him, grinning.

"I like it when you're on your back."

"I like it when you're straddling me," he said. "Fire again, to convince him." Slocum peered around the woman to where Montague watched. "He's still suspicious."

"He'll be more than that if he doesn't lead us to the silver." Tamara pointed the pistol at a dirt clump and fired. A tiny puff of smoke and dust rose.

Slocum fought to keep from sneezing. He kicked once and lay still.

"There," Tamara said loudly. "That takes care of him."

"Where are your horses?" Montague asked.

"Mine is down the line a ways. I don't know where his went. I rode around separate from him."

Montague shifted his weight from foot to foot, as if undecided what to do next. Then he said, "In a draw, not too far off. I left them there when I climbed the hill to take a potshot at you."

"I forgive you, now that we are partners. Come along. I'll get my horse."

Tamara herded him along to where her horse pawed the ground. It took a few seconds to gentle the horse after it had gotten all het up from the gunfire. She mounted, looked down at Montague, and said, "Let's get your horses and retrieve the silver."

"There is time if the railroad isn't sending anyone to take it away for a week."

"You know Collingswood. He might have a fire lit under him and will send out men sooner than that."

"I don't know him. That was Jackson's part."

"And mine," Tamara reminded him.

She rode behind as he circled the hill. Two horses had been hobbled in a ravine. Montague released both, and hopped bareback onto one.

"This is the easier one to ride without a saddle." He rode closer to Tamara. When the other horse reared and distracted Tamara, Montague leaned over and shoved her from her horse. Tamara hit the ground hard, shaken.

"So long," Montague called. He snared the dangling reins on her horse and hopped from bareback into the saddle. He settled down. "I hate bareback. Now I have tack—and three horses!"

Tamara sat up and drew her pistol.

"You can't do this to me!" She fired, missing him when the outlaw ducked. She fired repeatedly until she came up empty. With the two she had shot at Slocum, the remaining five all sang off wildly to urge Montague on his way.

Slocum rode up on his mare when Montague was out of sight. He laughed at how indignant Tamara looked.

"He stole my horse!"

"We wanted him to escape," Slocum pointed out. "With you along, he'd never go to the silver. Why needlessly split his loot with an interloper? Now he thinks he has two packhorses."

"He stole my horse!"

Slocum reached down and waited for Tamara to take his hand. She did so, and he pulled her up behind him. The mare sagged under the additional weight but plodded on. Now that Slocum had a fresh trail, one marked by three horses, he had no trouble tracking Montague.

"How much of a lead should we give him?" Tamara asked. She rested her cheek against Slocum's shoulder and clung around his waist.

"You don't sound in too much of a hurry to catch him," Slocum said. For his own part, he liked the feel of her arms circling him and the way she pressed into him from behind.

"How far do you think he got with his share after the robbery? Jack carried his almost ten miles."

"We don't know what Jackson did with his," he reminded her. "That map of his was worthless."

"It meant something."

"Only to Jackson." Slocum settled down and let the mare choose the gait. If they closed too soon with Montague, they'd spook him. The outlaw had no reason to think anyone was on his trail. Slocum ought to have been dead and Tamara left on foot. "If I was him, I'd ride fast a mile or two, then slow down, maybe check my back trail, then make a beeline for the silver."

"Do you think Harry and Riley are anywhere near?"

Slocum had no answer to that. He had been thinking more about Montague and the silver than the two specials. They had lit out after the other two train robbers. There was no telling where they had gone. He thought little of their skills, but even a blind squirrel found an acorn now and then. If the robbers got careless, the specials could have boxed them in or followed them to the silver.

"John, the bend in the canyon. Be careful."

He saw what had alerted her. Tamara hadn't been as content to ride along heedless of her surroundings as he'd thought. He had laid out how he would have sought the silver if he were Montague, and this was a perfect spot to lie in wait for anyone on his back trail. Slocum drew rein and studied the area. The sun was sinking fast now, but the long shadows cast betrayed Montague. The man stood just beyond the bend in the canyon.

Slocum got his bearings. The mountainous terrain had been hell for the railroad. Steep-walled canyons made travel even by horse difficult. Wrestling the stolen silver this far would have shown more determination than he expected from the robbers, though the sheer number of silver bars would feed their greed and push them to extraordinary lengths.

"He's running, John. Look!"

Slocum saw the shadow lengthen and then turn thin as Montague rode away fast. The sound of hoofbeats reached him a few seconds later.

"What are we going to do?" Tamara asked. "He knows we're on him like flies on shit."

Slocum looked over his shoulder and wondered about her. Most times she presented herself as a high-class lady. A thief, true, and one capable of shooting down a man without too many qualms, but she spoke well and comported herself with just a touch of haughtiness to show she was better than everyone around her. Then she said something like she just had.

"We can't let him ride off. We'd never find him if he decided to hide out." Slocum was still galled by how Montague had abandoned the wagon and eluded his best tracking.

He urged the tired mare to a fast walk. To trot or even gallop was out of the question with two riders. Slocum considered asking Tamara to drop off—or even knocking her off—to go after Montague. The idea disappeared when they reached the bend in the canyon. A loud screech of utter terror echoed back to them.

"What made that sound?" Tamara spoke in a low voice that quavered with emotion. "I've never heard anything like it."

"A horse," Slocum said. He urged the mare to more speed. The canyon opened onto another steep drop-off.

Two horses neighed and backed from the verge. One was Tamara's horse, still saddled but without the rider.

"Where's Montague?"

"Get your horse. And the other one," Slocum said.

He dismounted, secured the reins with a rock, and went

to the top of the cliff. The story cut into the dirt and rock told him what he would find. For whatever reason, Montague had either been pulled off Tamara's horse or had tried to jump over to ride one of his bareback.

Slocum peered over the edge. Darkness hid most of the jagged rock on the wall, but a single ray of sunlight sneaked through to spotlight a dead horse and mangled rider eighty feet below.

As Tamara came over, he said, "I found Montague."

He tried to keep her from looking but failed. She let out a gasp and turned to bury her face in his shoulder. He held her. She wasn't crying, but from the way she shook, he knew what went through her mind. That could have been them below.

Instead she said, "Now we'll never find the silver."

14

"Do you think he has a map to the silver?" Tamara pushed back and looked up at Slocum. "Jack had one."

"For all the good that did us. From what you said about Jackson, he needed it to find where he hid it, getting everything turned around the way he did. Montague didn't have any reason to make a map, for himself or anyone else."

"The other two robbers might have needed to know where he hid all their shares."

Slocum shook his head. None of that made sense after seeing Montague.

"The three weren't partners, not like that. Montague was on his own. Drury and Baldy might be pulling on the same yoke, but Jackson, like Montague, was on his own."

"I suppose you're right. Where does that leave us?" Tamara tried to look back over the brink but the sun had sunk lower, plunging the entire ravine below into deep shadow. "He *might* have made a map."

"I'm not going down there to find out," Slocum said. "But that doesn't mean Montague didn't steal your horse and ride toward the spot where he did hide his share from the robbery."

"It's around here?" Tamara looked into the gathering darkness. "Where?"

"Not in the ravine with Montague," Slocum said. "He had no way of hiding the silver there. It'd make no sense to just dump it over the side where anyone could see it."

"It would have shone like the sun itself," Tamara agreed. "So it's up here?"

"There are caves in the mountains. The canyon approaching this point had crevices where he could stuff a lot of silver bars." Slocum slowly turned, keeping his arm around Tamara's waist to move her from the edge of the precipice. "Farther along this trail," Slocum said, his voice going low.

"Let's look! Come on, John. We can find it. You've got to be right."

Tamara pulled free and hurried to her horse. She mounted and set off, not waiting for him. He knew finding where Montague had hidden his silver in the dark was nigh on impossible. He retrieved his mare but only walked it, tugging occasionally on the reins to keep the horse from munching at patches of succulent grass. In less than ten minutes he found Tamara, sitting on her horse and sobbing.

"I don't know what to do, John. It's got to be here somewhere. You said so yourself. But where? Where?"

He got her off the horse and said softly, "We'll find it in the morning. We don't have a ghost of a chance in the dark."

Doubts rose they would have any better chance after sunup. But that was all they could do unless giving up was in the cards. For Slocum, it wasn't. One look at how distraught Tamara was over not finding the silver told him they were not riding back to San Francisco anytime soon.

"It's been hours, John. We're no closer to finding the silver than we were this morning."

He realized they had been following the canyon and had

curved back toward the railroad tracks. That spoke to how rugged the region was and how difficult it was not to get lost in the winding, intersecting canyons. The twin steel ribbons clung tenaciously to the side of a mountain with only occasional widening for meadows or narrow canyons leading deep into the range. As frustrating as it was when he saw they had come full circle and returned to the tracks, it also heartened him. None of the robbers had planned ahead and knew less about the terrain than he did. When they had to hide the bulk of their ill-gotten gains, they took the first place that they found because they hadn't brought freight wagons—Tamara hadn't realized the size of the shipment and neither had the gang. Jackson had been the smartest of the robbers, from what Slocum could tell, and his success in hiding came more from his disability than cleverness.

"Montague rode where he did because he'd stashed his cut along that trail," Slocum said. "We ought to go back along it and—"

He clamped his mouth shut when gunshots rang out.

"What's happening, John?" Tamara reached for her small pistol, then hesitated when she saw a half-dozen men riding along the tracks, coming over the summit. The lead rider wore a badge pinned to his chest.

"We haven't done anything. Don't rile the posse," he cautioned.

He touched the papers in his coat pocket detailing how he worked for the Central California Railroad. Unless Collingswood had put out the word that he had fired him, Slocum knew this would carry some weight.

"Who're you?" The deputy halted his posse and eyed Slocum and Tamara.

Slocum allowed a tiny smile to come to his lips. The lawman wasted no time on Slocum but gave Tamara an appraising look. She shifted in the saddle and graced the man with a hint of ankle to keep him diverted.

"Why, Marshal, we're Mr. Collingswood's assistants. He's vice president of this railroad, you know."

"We know. He's the one what put out a big reward for the capture of the robbers. You prove you're who you say?"

"How many of the train robbers were ladies?" Tamara gave a light laugh meant to disarm any suspicion. "You don't believe I'm one of those thugs, do you, Marshal?"

"I'm only a deputy, and no, ma'am, I don't. What about your companion?"

"I've got a warrant signed by Mr. Collingswood," Slocum said. "You want to see it?"

The deputy did. Slocum slowly pulled the now tattered sheet of paper from his coat pocket, aware than two of the posse had hands on their six-shooters and the rest watched him with the same attention they'd give a coiled diamondback. He rode closer and let the lawman read it. The man's lips moved as he worked down the page, but when Slocum saw him mouthing "David Collingswood," he knew the document still carried some weight.

"Looks all right to me," the deputy said, handing back the sheet to Slocum. "You scouting around for the outlaws, too?"

"Tell me, Marshal—excuse me, Deputy—have you encountered any other specials sent by Mr. Collingswood?" Tamara batted her eyes at the man.

Slocum appreciated how he might as well not even exist. It gave him anonymity if the deputy was the kind to leaf through wanted posters. Slocum's face appeared on enough for him to be recognizable. But more than this, it gave him a chance to let his mare edge closer to the others in the posse so he could hear what they were whispering among themselves.

They fell silent as Slocum came near. He asked, "You see any trace of the robbers?"

"None," said one man, small, intense, and with the look of a bounty hunter. He carried two pistols slung in cross-draw holsters, a bandolier crammed with ammunition, and a large-caliber Sharps rifle tucked into his saddle scabbard. The usual member of a posse recruited from a saloon wouldn't be this heavily armed.

"I spotted a couple fellows not too long back." Slocum described Riley and Harry. "From the way they skulked around, well, it was mighty suspicious."

"Ain't seen them," the small man said.

"You ought to get on back to Frisco," the deputy called to Slocum, breaking off what had turned into an intimate discussion with Tamara. "It can get mighty dangerous if we corner those owlhoots." He turned back to Tamara and said, "We wouldn't want anything to happen to you."

"Why, no, Deputy, we wouldn't." She graced him with a winning smile. "Why, you might see fit to take me to the Union Club if you earn that reward. I'd like that."

"So would I, ma'am, so would I." The deputy cleared his throat and got his posse trotting back upslope toward the summit.

Tamara waved to the man when he turned around to see if she was watching.

"We've got to hurry, John," she said, still smiling and waving. "The deputy said at least one more posse had been sent out from Fremont."

"I asked about Riley and Harry, but they hadn't spotted them. I'm more worried that Collingswood ordered more specials to cover the area." Slocum chewed on his lower lip as he studied the terrain downslope where the robbery had occurred.

"They're riding around, making a whale of a lot of noise and feeling good about being paid a dollar a day," she said. "They want to return a week's pay richer with a story to brag on."

Slocum said nothing about the bounty hunter riding with the posse. Most of the deputized citizens of San Francisco might think they rode out with visions of an easy five dollars promised them. Ten, if they took their time. But the intense bounty hunter had other game in his sights. He wanted both the gang of thieves and the silver. He wanted to hit the jackpot because that was what he did for a living.

"Montague wasn't sure where he was riding when he stole your horse," Slocum said. "Not exactly, but he knew the general direction. When we spooked him, we thought he'd stopped to ambush us. What if he'd stopped to fetch the silver?"

"We rode around in a circle and came back. We should have backtracked. John, that must be it!" She bent over and tried to kiss him but their horses refused to cooperate. Her kiss missed by a fraction of an inch. She laughed, then galloped away.

Slocum trailed behind, keeping up the best he could. His mare wasn't as fast as Tamara's horse, and he hung back to see if her reckless rush caused anyone to take notice. The men hunting for the silver were likely to take a shot at her. Slocum wanted to be in a position to defend her if that happened.

They left the railroad tracks and cut through the canyon. It took less time now to reach the canyon's bend than before since they weren't wary of Montague spotting them before he reached his cache.

"Wait up," Slocum called. "Tamara, wait."

"What is it, John? I want to hunt before the sun goes down. We had that problem yesterday."

"Someone's up there. Listen."

Rocks fell in a small cascade down the side of the mountain. The echo reached them in time for Tamara to check her headlong advance and let Slocum catch up. He touched the ebony butt of his pistol, then decided his rifle might be a better choice. Pulling it from its sheath, he motioned for her to stay as he explored around the bend in the canyon.

Barely had he rounded the sharp angle than he saw two horses tethered and impatiently tugging, trying to get away from the dust and commotion higher on the slope.

Slocum swung his rifle up, only to find he was in Riley's sights.

"Did you find something?" Slocum called. "The silver from the shipment?"

"Maybe we did and maybe we didn't," the special said. "Whatever we did, it's all ours."

"If it's the stolen silver bars, it belongs to the Central California Railroad," Slocum said. He saw Harry move around a rock. His rifle came up to cover Slocum, too.

Slocum knew he was a better shot than either man. Even outnumbered, he could take out one and have a decent shot at the other before they hit him. His problem lay in them being on solid ground while his mare crow-hopped around under him. Then the dilemma of whether to shoot or back off got worse. Tamara joined him.

"They found it, didn't they? It's those two from Newburg."

"Well, lookee there," Riley said. "If it ain't the lady from town what engaged us so entertaining-like."

"They'll open fire if we don't back off," Slocum said in a low voice, but Tamara paid no attention.

"You two were hired by Mr. Collingswood. I know because I approved your employment. I am his personal assistant."

"You a secretary?" Harry stepped out to get a better look at her.

"I am," Tamara said. "I will put in a good word with not only Mr. Collingswood but the president of the Central California Railroad, as well. I am well known to both men."

Riley and Harry moved closer and exchanged a few hot words. Riley finally turned back and called, "Why don't you and this galoot head on back to San Francisco? Me and Harry will see to assembling the loot and returning it to the depot."

"All four of us can make the work go ever so much faster," Tamara said. Before Slocum could protest, she whispered to him, "Leave them alone with the silver and they'll steal it. Dammit, it's *ours!*"

"Let them pack it up, then we can take it," Slocum said.

He was immediately overruled when Riley motioned for them to ride closer. Slocum worried the specials wanted them where the killing shots wouldn't be as difficult. Neither of them had the look of a decent marksman.

Slocum was keyed up and jumpy. Tamara rode confidently. All he could think of was either of the specials taking it into his head to kill both of them and remove any chance that the silver had to be returned.

"Is this the share of the loot hidden by Pierre Montague?"

Both specials stared at Tamara.

"He wasn't the one we was huntin'."

"You lost both Baldy and Drury," Slocum said, guessing what had happened. "How did you come on the cache?"

"We're both skilled trackers. We seen rocks what had been moved and—"

"Shut up, Harry," said Riley. "Don't go givin' away our secret skills."

"Yes, I see what you mean," Tamara said. "You two were clever to notice how those rocks were piled in front of the cave. Why, less skilled scouts than you would have ridden past, thinking it was only the remnant of an avalanche." She cast a sidelong accusing look at Slocum.

"Is it the entire shipment or only a quarter?" Slocum asked.

He should have kept his mouth shut. Both men turned their rifles trained on him. He rested his hand on his six-gun, glad now for the diminished distance. Even against two rifles, he put more faith in his trusty Colt Navy. It was about the best six-shooter for getting off the first accurate shot. Take out one—Riley was nearest—and the other would hesitate. He doubted either of these men had ever been in combat with rifles firing and artillery erupting. A shot would cause the surviving man to jump.

"Yes, sir, that is one smart example of hunting," came a cold voice. "I compliment you boys on finding the stolen silver."

A shot ripped through the air, startling not only the specials but Slocum and Tamara as well.

15

"Who the hell're you?" Riley demanded. He swung his rifle around in the bounty hunter's direction. The small, intense man ignored the special, focused on Slocum.

"The deputy and the rest of the posse aren't too far away," the bounty hunter said. He directed his words to Slocum again, not the specials. He had sized up his opposition well.

Slocum saw how Riley and Harry exchanged a look that meant death for the bounty hunter. Then their resolve faded when the man whipped out his second pistol and covered both men. Riley and Harry might not be too bright, but they read death in the bounty hunter's eyes.

Then the moment cracked apart, and the tension changed as the deputy galloped up with the rest of the posse trailing behind.

"You catch the robbers, Trey?"

"Think not," the bounty hunter said. "I do think the stolen silver's up there."

"You was spyin' on us!" Harry's outrage boiled over. He lifted his rifle, ignoring Trey leveling both pistols on him.

"I'm U.S. Deputy Marshal Ford, and I'm ordering you to lower that rifle. Do it now or die on the spot."

"He's a lawman, Harry. Don't cross him." Riley pushed his partner's rifle down.

"Uh, Riley, they's gonna take the silver."

"We are returning it to the railroad. Mr. Collingswood's personal representatives will vouch for us." The deputy cast a hard look at Slocum for the briefest instant before lingering on Tamara. "We can have the silver moved and loaded on the afternoon train and back in a vault before nightfall."

"We can take custody of the silver, if you prefer, Deputy Ford." Tamara turned on all her charm, but Slocum saw that the lawman was impervious to it now that the silver was within reach.

"You aren't in line for any reward, ma'am, not if your salary's being paid by the railroad. The men riding with me depend on that reward to make their sacrifice of time and life worthwhile."

"What 'bout us? We was hired to find the silver," protested Riley. "We're paid, jist like you, Deputy, but there was supposed to be a reward. And we was the ones what found where the robbers hid the damned silver."

"He poses a good question. What about it, ma'am?"

Slocum cut in before Tamara could speak.

"If Riley and Harry returned with the silver, there's no reason why Mr. Collingswood wouldn't personally give them the reward promised."

The two specials exchanged looks. Harry started to argue, but Riley cut him off with a hand motion like chopping wood.

"We kin guard the silver 'gainst another robbery," Riley said. "That suit you fellows?"

"It is an admirable solution. You and the posse can all collect your reward. Be sure to tell Mr. Collingswood that I approved the payment."

"You aren't going back with the silver?" The deputy pinned Tamara with his gimlet stare.

"Mr. Slocum and I are tending to railroad business away from San Francisco."

"What business is that?" Deputy Ford refused to let the matter drop.

"When you talk to Mr. Collingswood, he will tell you, if he sees fit to divulge such things to someone outside the company."

Slocum almost laughed at Tamara's response. It was perfect. He had been quick enough to force Riley and Harry back to San Francisco and out of their hair while they hunted for the rest of the silver. Jackson's was lost and now Montague's share was on its way back to the railroad's coffers. Half the silver was still hidden and waiting to be found.

Waiting to be found by him and Tamara.

"Yup, Trey, this is the shipment." A posse member poked his head out of a shallow cave and held up a dull silver bar. "Couple hundred of these in here."

"That's the railroad's stolen shipment," Tamara said hurriedly. She left the impression it was all that had been stolen.

"All right, boys. Each of you take a bar in turn until it's all gone. I'll be counting so don't you figure on taking one or two for your troubles. The reward's going to be your payment."

Slocum and Tamara watched from the top of a boulder as the posse moved the bars out. Slocum saw Tamara's lips moving as she counted. Of everyone here, she knew the exact number of silver bars stolen, from the report given to Collingswood.

"You sure you don't want to catch that train and ride back to San Francisco?"

"Thanks, Deputy, but we're on other business," Slocum said.

"I'll mention you and the lady," Deputy Ford said. "Straight to that vice president."

"Tell Mr. Collingswood I'll complete the railroad business within the week and be back at my desk soon," Tamara said.

Slocum watched the lawman's reaction. Ford remained skeptical, but Trey ran his fingers nervously over the butts of his six-shooters. Nothing Tamara had said convinced the bounty hunter, but staying with the silver outweighed everything else.

Riley and Harry trailed the posse, arguing over what to do. Slocum caught snippets of their dispute. Then the posse, specials, and silver disappeared around the bend in the canyon. He waited a few more minutes before saying to Tamara, "They won't go back with the silver. They know this isn't the entire shipment."

"Those two are smarter than they look, then. I counted the bars. This was a quarter of the entire shipment. They want to get rid of the posse and keep looking for the rest."

"Just like us," Slocum said.

"Half is lost to us. What do you think about Baldy and Drury and their shares?"

Slocum sucked on his teeth as he considered the matter. While Montague had occupied him most recently, the other two outlaws presented a different problem.

"Might be they stored their cut together," he said. "Drury isn't able to make off with as much silver as Ford and his posse took away from the cave. With help from Baldy, he could take his share."

"Opium saps a man's strength. I saw how he looked, all pale and shaking. Drury is closer to death than life."

"I wouldn't put it past Baldy to try to steal all of it, but the two might be real partners. From what I saw back in Newburg, Baldy's not going to double-cross him."

"Half of a mountain is a whale of a lot of silver, John. Where do we look?"

"The specials trailed Baldy and Drury but found Montague's silver," he said, thinking aloud. "The two outlaws lost them somewhere. I don't know Baldy, but Drury wasn't feebleminded. While he was all hopped up, he played poker with a vengeance and only lost because he was being cheated by a pair of gamblers working together."

"That's not so bright," Tamara said, scowling.

"He thinks he has an unlimited supply of silver bars."

Slocum touched the one still riding in his pocket and felt mixed emotions. He thrilled at being this rich after so many months of being down on his luck, but greed intruded itself. If he found the outlaws' cache, he would be richer than any but the titans of industry and railroad in San Francisco.

"Riley and Harry aren't going back to San Francisco, are they?"

Slocum shook his head. Somehow, they'd try to get their cut of the reward for finding Montague's cache, but the lure of the remaining loot had to be overwhelming. Slocum knew what he felt, and he wasn't a greedy man. Or not as greedy as those two. And Tamara. Her eyes shone like tiny suns whenever she spoke of the silver.

"They'll let Ford and the others escort the silver they found back to San Francisco and keep looking for the robbers."

"And the silver," Tamara finished.

Slocum stepped up into the saddle and waited for Tamara to mount. Without a word he rode off, with her trotting behind as he went directly to the railroad tracks. This stretch had seen more traffic on horseback than it had from engines and the attached cars rattling along its length. As he neared the rails, the ground began shaking. He stopped and pointed. He and Tamara watched as the train from Virginia City struggled to make a turn and then start up the steep grade to the summit.

The engineer leaned out of the cab, spotted the posse ahead, and barked orders to his brakeman. Not having to throw coal into the boiler, the brakeman leaned out to see what the engineer already had.

"What a terrible job," Tamara said. "Straining to shovel coal or wood all day, covered in soot and blasted by heat from the boiler."

"Robbing a train is easier," Slocum allowed. Tamara looked at him, startled, then laughed.

"Let's hope we can profit from the crimes of others."

Slocum agreed. The train ground a halt amid sparks flying from its steel wheels. The cars were hidden from view, but Slocum heard Deputy Ford and the posse begin loading the silver into a freight car, then joining their metallic treasure by jumping their horses in. When the screeching of steel against steel warned of the departure, Slocum kicked at his mare's flanks and got onto the tracks behind the train.

"Did the specials board, too?" Tamara asked.

"They aren't waiting alongside the tracks. That must mean they are taking the road along the cliff where Montague took a header."

"Do we follow or head them off?" Tamara looked behind them, in the direction of the canyon where the silver had been discovered. "Backtracking means the same scenery as before. Frankly, I am sick of this part of the mountains along the tracks."

"We were thorough," Slocum said. "Let's go farther down the tracks and take a branch neither Jackson nor Montague rode. We can camp and wait for Riley and Harry."

"If we miss them like you did Montague and the wagon? What then?"

Slocum's anger flared a moment. He tamped it down. Not seeing the abandoned wagon had been careless, but Montague had been spurred to take desperate action.

"Then we have to work harder to outthink them," he said. "That shouldn't be too hard."

"No, it shouldn't," Tamara said, her gaze lingering on him.

Slocum trotted along the tracks until he found a decent-sized canyon leading to the south. Montague had taken the first one to the north and Jackson had gone farther east before turning north to hide his silver. If Baldy and Drury were heavily burdened and the hophead wasn't doing his share of the work, this canyon made sense.

Slocum rode along, studying the walls. The canyon floor was U-shaped rather than cut into a deep V like the others. He didn't see as many potential hiding places here.

"John, look."

He had concentrated so much on hiding places that he had neglected to watch where they rode. Tamara had found a fresh pile of horse manure. From the flies and way it had only partly hardened, the horse responsible for leaving it behind couldn't be more than a half hour ahead.

"It's not the specials," Slocum said. "They'd be behind us unless they're riding Fourth of July rockets."

Tamara caught her breath. They were closing in on the outlaws or another posse. Collingswood had sent out as many men as he could to recover the shipment. But which of all those groups rode ahead of them?

"Can you tell from the tracks how many riders there are?"

"The rocky ground makes it hard to identify hoofprints," Slocum admitted. "There might be three or four."

Gunshots rang out ahead of them. Slocum made a quick decision.

"Stay back, let me see what's happening."

"Like hell I will!"

Tamara galloped ahead, forcing Slocum to match her pace. He bent low and tried to look ahead even as he watched the ground flying by under his mare's hooves. By the time the shooting stopped, he still had no idea how many men they'd face.

"Tamara, wait!" He pulled his horse to a halt amid flying stones and sparks of horseshoes grating against rock. "I need to scout. Stay with the horses."

He tossed her his reins and hit the ground, stumbled, and caught himself to rush forward. She cursed him but remained behind. He knew they would die if they blundered ahead and found themselves facing another posse. Rapid gunfire followed by silence meant the fight had been fierce and ended abruptly. Someone might have surrendered, but he doubted that. More likely, someone lay stretched out dead on the ground.

Moving low, Slocum worked his way forward through a stand of trees until he found a meadow on the far side. He dropped to his belly and waited for ten minutes to see if anyone stirred. When he saw no sign of life, he crept forward until the acrid stink of gun smoke made his nostrils flare. Sniffing, he homed in on the spot where the gunfight had been. The air was deathly still and a quirk of the canyon walls held the odor in place, waiting for a brisk wind to send it on its way.

A body lay facedown at the edge of a pond. Slocum drew his six-gun and went forward. He didn't see anyone else. Whoever had shot the man had fled. When he got close enough, he saw that Baldy wasn't going to spill his guts about the silver's hiding place. He had already spilled his guts after a dozen bullets had ripped into his belly.

Slocum went to the pond, dipped his finger in it, and sniffed. No sulfur. A quick taste showed him it was sweet water. He plunged his head into the water. Refreshed, he pulled back and shook like a dog, then scooped up the water to kill his thirst.

The sounds of horses didn't surprise him. Tamara hadn't obeyed. She rode straight for him, his mare trotting along behind.

"That's one of the robbers," she said rather than asked.

"Baldy."

"Who killed him?"

"It had to be Riley and Harry. They must have made an excuse to Ford and ridden off before we got there."

"So they didn't circle back along the cliff where Montague died?"

"Two riders, three horses." Slocum pointed to the south where they had ridden.

"They wouldn't have killed him unless they knew where he had stashed the silver." Tamara dropped to the ground and knelt by the pond, delicately splashing water on her face and neck rather than plunging her head in the way Slocum had.

"He might not have given them a choice, but the amount of lead they pumped into him says that they didn't much want to take him alive."

"That means they knew where he hid the . . . silver."

Slocum looked at her when her words trailed off. She put both hands on the muddy bank, then plunged her head underwater the way he had. Only she didn't surface. She kept her head under so long she began blowing bubbles. Just as Slocum started to pull her back, she exploded from the water. A huge grin lighted up her face.

"I know where the silver was. In the pond!"

Slocum shoved his head underwater and this time kept his eyes open. When he surfaced, he said, "You're right. Baldy dumped the silver in the pool. But it's gone now."

The smile on Tamara's face faded as she realized he was right.

16

"Who took it? It hasn't been gone long. Even I can see how it was dragged out from the water."

"The bars left deep holes," Slocum said. The water hadn't erased the outlines of the removed bars yet. Hiding it underwater showed how clever Baldy had been. Rather than finding a cave where others might look, he had dumped the crates into the water, effectively hiding them from view. If the water was the least bit muddy, no one would ever spot the silver.

The calm wind and the still, warm day had settled the mud and made it crystalline. Finding the crates had been easy for whoever rode off with the silver.

"It has to be Riley and Harry," said Tamara. "If it had been another posse with a lawman, we would have met them as they came out with the silver, ready to send it back to San Francisco, just like Montague's."

Slocum walked around, studying the tracks. Three horses. He should have studied the hoofprints left by the specials' horses to find nicks or loose nails. That small sign would have given him positive identification now with the perfect imprints in the soft ground around the pond.

"It doesn't matter who killed Baldy and took the silver. We can overtake them. Their horses are heavily loaded."

"Heavy enough to account for half the silver?"

"I don't know," he told the woman. "If the silver Deputy Ford shipped back is any indication, I don't think this amounts to much more."

"Or any more? You're saying Baldy and Drury didn't hide their shares together?"

"Drury might be the one who shot down Baldy, but I don't think so. There were too many gunshots for one man to be gunning down another." He kicked at spent brass all around. Baldy had been shot a dozen times or more by two different rifles. If it had been Drury's doing, he carried a powerful hate for his partner that Slocum hadn't seen. "Still, opium can rot a man's mind and make him do things he would never consider otherwise."

"Baldy might have denied him the drug," said Tamara. "Addicts get violent when deprived." She bent and scooped palm after palm laden with water into her mouth.

"You done drinking? The horses have had their fill. We've got some silver to retrieve."

Tamara let out a joyous whoop and clambered into the saddle, her skirts flying about as she settled down. Slocum had to ride hard to catch up with her, but by the time they left the meadow and once more walked their horses along a rocky stretch, she had calmed down.

"If Baldy didn't hide Drury's share, that means we can get as much as half the shipment all for ourselves," she said.

Slocum kept his eyes on the ground, only occasionally glancing up to be sure they weren't riding into an ambush. If anything, they found themselves in terrain once more turning dangerous with steep cliffs showing up where valleys ought to be. For the riders ahead, this meant a slower pace. Even better, the bends around the sheer rock faces cut off a view of their back trail. Slocum thought they could sneak up almost unseen on the riders ahead.

"John, ahead. See?"

He squinted in time to see a horse tail flicking back and forth before vanishing around an angle. The drop-off to the right grew from a few yards to what Slocum estimated to be a hundred feet. The rush of a river told him why this deep ravine had formed.

"I'll get as close as I can, then—"

"Listen. Do you hear that?"

A train whistle blasted through the silence. Tamara twisted about, getting her bearings.

"We're not far from the railroad tracks again, but this time we're several miles to the east. This trail curls back toward the tracks. It has to."

"If the riders in front of us hadn't known that before, they do now."

Another blast from the steam whistle died down. Slocum fancied he could hear the powerful engine and the grating of wheels against rails.

"That must be a limited. The deputy and his posse took the scheduled train back to San Francisco. This one must be highballing it through from Sacramento. That doesn't happen often, but when it does, the train usually carries legislators or even the governor."

"Will it overtake the train with the silver?"

Tamara shook her head.

"Once at the summit, the other train can steam ahead at full pressure. They might arrive at the depot about the same time, but this one's not going to run into the other. Why does it matter? Do you think if there's a crash, we could loot the silver?"

Slocum had to hand it to the woman. She had a one-track mind. Her need to steal the railroad's metal had to have a deep motivation. His own was simpler. David Collingswood had insulted him, impugned his good nature, and both the man and the company deserved to pay for it. Losing the silver would not sit well with his board of directors. Slocum took some satisfaction in the chance that Collingswood would be fired and thrown out into the street.

However, he knew men like that always landed on their feet. A vice president for a major railroad, no matter how bad his errors in judgment, always found another job without too long a wait. Mingle a bit among the wealthy residing on Russian Hill and go to a smoker or two and the Central California Railroad's competitors would make him a job offer. The only real satisfaction Slocum would get had to be recovering the silver and keeping it.

"The train's stopped. Do you hear, John?"

He craned his head around but didn't hear what the woman insisted to be the truth. Then he jumped as the whistle let out three long blasts. The train's rattle faded quickly.

"It stopped, then built up a head of steam, and is heading on into Oakland."

"Why would it stop?" Even as Slocum asked the question, an answer popped up and turned him cold inside.

The train had let someone off. Or worse, it might have taken on passengers.

"Not that," Tamara said, reading his mind. "The men ahead of us are too far from the tracks to get aboard the train."

"Then another posse might be waiting for the men with the silver."

Both of them kicked at their horses' flanks and shot off, but Slocum had to rein back and slow to a walk when the trail turned into another of the treacherous ledges along the top of a cliff. He called to Tamara to slow down, but the woman pushed ahead. Cursing under his breath, he dismounted and walked his horse, thinking this was safer than riding should the mare stumble. Pressed against the rocky wall, he followed the trail around a sharp bend and was relieved to see it opened onto a rocky area that stretched forward to the eastern pass where the Central California Railroad had laid its tracks.

His relief passed like a feather blown away in a tornado when he saw that Tamara had caught up with Riley and Harry. The specials were unlimbering their rifles to shoot her out of the saddle as she galloped toward them. At this range any shot Slocum made would be wasted. He tried anyway.

Pulling his Winchester out, he judged distances, elevated the muzzle to arc the bullet since a flat trajectory was out of the question, and then he fired. The bullet sailed too high but still got a result he could be proud of. Riley's horse reared, forcing him to lower his rifle. As the horse danced around, spooked by Slocum's bullet, the special banged into his partner.

Tamara coming to her senses and realizing she was outgunned was too much to hope for. She rushed forward. Her arm swept out and hit Harry in the shoulder, adding further confusion to the one-sided fight. Slocum had no choice but to join the fray. He vaulted up and got as much speed from his horse as he could. He kept the rifle snugged into his shoulder and fired, but his shots all went wide since he didn't want to accidentally hit Tamara. She and Riley were locked in a fight on horseback.

He swung his rifle around and clipped her on the side of the head. She tumbled to the ground. Slocum fired faster now that the woman wasn't blocking either of the men. His shots came close but only frightened the horses. He stopped firing when he saw that Tamara was rolling and dodging the horses' flying hooves. Both specials' horses reared and pawed at the air before coming down hard only inches from her.

The men got their mounts under control. For a brief instant Slocum hoped Tamara could escape. When new firing came, it took Slocum a second to realize what danger he was in. The lead sailed past him—and past both specials.

From the direction of the railroad tracks charged four men, all firing.

"Stay down!" His warning to Tamara went unheeded. She was on her feet, trying to get out her .22 rimfire pistol.

Slocum found himself caught between Riley and Harry as they tried to escape the posse. In close quarters, he swung his rifle. It cracked against Riley's, lifted to deflect the blow. Slocum tried to twist around and grab the man but lost his balance. He crashed to the ground. His rifle fell some distance away. Stunned, he tried to get to his feet, but Harry caught him with a boot in the back of the head.

Stunned, Slocum dropped facedown again. Bees buzzed in his head, and everywhere he looked turned double. He fumbled out his Colt as he rolled onto his back. Deciding which image to shoot at proved impossible. He shot at both blurry Rileys above him, first left, then right. From the gasp of pain, one had been a successful shot.

Then Slocum stared up into the blue California sky. A puffy white cloud tried to sneak over a distant mountain peak. He tried to hold back the laugh when he saw how much it looked like David Collingswood. Then he sagged back to the ground and closed his eyes. Red pain filled his skull. When he opened his eyes, he saw a familiar face.

"Didn't think I'd find you out here, son," Underwood said.

"Just trying to do the job I was hired to do." Slocum sat up and laid his six-shooter in his lap.

"You leave that piece where it is. Don't go reachin' for it."

Slocum looked up. His vision cleared enough to see that Underwood held a scattergun in his good left hand. It was aimed smack at Slocum.

"You're after the wrong one," Slocum said. "The two specials tried to steal the silver shipment for themselves."

"As if that thought didn't dance through your brain, just for a second or two. And you might be goin' 'round tellin' folks you work for the railroad after Mr. Collingswood fired you." Underwood looked over his shoulder. "Her, too. That's a pity. Miss Crittenden prettied up the office and made goin' to see Mr. Collingswood worthwhile."

"You came on the train from the east?"

"Me and the boys was over in Sacramento runnin' down a lead on the stolen silver. Heard tell of a big spender shovin' silver bars across the poker table like they was dollar chips. Turned out to be a wild-goose chase."

"You'd better get to flying if you want to catch those two geese." Slocum jerked his thumb behind him.

"John, they got away with the silver!"

"Miss Crittenden, good to see you again." Underwood stared at the distraught woman with more than polite attention.

She looked down, saw her blouse had ripped away, exposing one breast. She hastily pulled up the torn cloth and struggled to hold it in place.

"Don't go doin' nothin' special for the likes of me," Underwood said.

"You're a dirty old man," she snapped.

"Can't deny the truth. Always was, always will be, I reckon, until the day I die." Underwood looked up as one from his posse trotted back.

"We got 'em both pinned down," the man reported. He looked at Slocum and Tamara. "These the two you was huntin'?"

"Any proof those two yonder got silver bars?" Underwood asked.

"That's why they couldn't get away. A packhorse and both their saddle horses goin' on swaybacked from the weight atop 'em. They're carryin' something heavy. Must be the railroad's silver."

"I agree," Underwood said. "Get on back and help Gus and Squinty. We'll be along in a few minutes."

Without another word, Underwood's man wheeled around and raced back to the fight. Sporadic gunfire told of the posse keeping the specials under cover and not allowing them to escape but still not inclined to make a real fight of it.

Underwood swung his shotgun around, pointed at the space between Tamara and Slocum. He heaved a deep sigh, used his mangled hand to swipe at sweat leaking from under his hatband, then finally said, "What am I gonna do with you two?"

"We—"

"Be quiet, Miss Crittenden. I was sent out here to bring you both in. Mr. Collingswood caught wind of you scramblin' around to find the silver and steal it. It wasn't me. I don't know where he heard that, but he did. The reward on your heads is danged near as big as on the actual robbers."

"He's got problems with the board of directors and wants to use us as scapegoats," Tamara said, ignoring how Underwood twisted slightly to cover her with the shotgun.

"Don't know about his woes, but you both have a world of trouble ahead if I take you back."

"Riley and Harry have what's left of the silver," Slocum said. "Give that to Collingswood. That'll make him forget all about us."

"Well, now, I don't know how that would work out. You sayin', Slocum, that what those two idiots stole is the remainder of the silver?"

"Deputy Ford put some on the train ahead of yours heading back to Oakland."

"Some?" Underwood perked up.

"They've got the rest," Slocum said, looking in the direction of increased gunfire. "They ran down Baldy and killed him."

"Baldy?"

Tamara hastily told of the four robbers and the trouble they had getting away with such a heavy burden.

"Mr. Collingswood thinks there was somebody in his office what told this Jackson fellow and the others about the shipment. You wouldn't know who that was, now would you, Miss Crittenden? Mr. Collingswood is comin' 'round to pointin' the finger at you to cover his own hiney. Seems he ignored Slocum's earlier accusation and wants to sweep it—and you both—under the rug."

"They're getting away," Slocum said. "Listen. The reports are dying down. That means your men have to get after them."

"Might mean Squinty shot 'em. Best damned sharp-shooter I ever did see, in spite of his name. Blind in one eye."

"The specials . . ." Tamara let her sentence trail off so Underwood could finish it.

"All right, you two. Mount up. We'll see how the fight's goin'. Don't take it into your heads to run."

"I want to see the silver," Tamara said wistfully.

Slocum and Tamara rode ahead of Underwood, aware of the shotgun aimed at their backs. They came to the edge of the trail inching around the side of the mountain. The rocky ledge had fallen down into the river below in places, making a direct assault on the two specials difficult.

"See what we're up against, boss?" The man peered up at Underwood, one eye screwed shut. "No way I kin get a good shot at either of 'em."

"How many places has that there rocky ledge collapsed?"

"Well, now, boss, when they led that packhorse of theirs across at least two sections, the trail done fell out from under its hooves."

"The horse," Tamara asked anxiously, "was it lost?"

"Think it was," Squinty said. "That mean there's no reason to keep after 'em?"

"I don't care if the silver's gone over the ledge," Underwood said. "I want them two owlhoots brought in."

"They're on the trail back around the end of this mountain," Squinty said. "We got to move on 'em fast."

"All right, Slocum," Underwood said. "You want to be a hero?"

Slocum took out his six-shooter, made sure he carried six loaded cylinders, and then kicked free to drop to the ground.

"He's using you, John. You'll get yourself killed."

"'Less I miss my guess, this ain't the first time Slocum's been ordered to do something like this," Underwood said.

"I'll be all right," Slocum said.

He wasn't sure if he reassured Tamara or threw it up into Underwood's face. Staying low, he worked to the trail and then to the first place where the trail had caved in. Cautiously looking over the edge, he saw a bloody smear on the rocks a dozen feet below, where the packhorse had hit first. The red trail extended another fifty feet down to the river. All along the cliff face he saw bright silver glints. The horse had died and in its death fall had scattered silver bars to the bottom of the ravine.

Facing the rock, he gathered his strength and launched himself across the three-foot break in the trail. He hit, caught himself, and worked farther along, hugging the stone to keep from becoming a target.

He fired off a round when he saw a hand with a six-gun poking out from around a rock. His bullet flew true, but the hand holding the gun only jerked with the impact. Slocum worked his way closer, knelt, and plucked the gun from nerveless fingers. A quick look showed that Harry no longer presented a threat. Slocum stepped past, not bothering to see how many slugs had taken the man's life. If Squinty was as a good a sniper as Underwood said, one bullet was all it took.

"Riley!" He shouted to the special to find where he was. "Your partner's dead. You will be, too, unless you give up."

His answer came in wild shots that sang off into the emptiness over the ravine. Riley fired wildly. Slocum listened hard but didn't hear a horse protesting the noise.

"You still have a horse to ride? The silver's lost. It's all in the river now."

This time not even gunfire came as a response. Slocum worked his way closer, found a bend in the trail, and whirled about, ready to shoot. There was no reason. Riley slumped against the rock face, six-shooter in his dead hand. Slocum looked over the edge of the cliff and caught his breath. At least one more horse had taken the plunge. The third horse was nowhere to be seen. It might have joined the other two in death after falling over the edge.

The specials were dead. And the silver they'd carried was lost.

17

"I got another one," Gus called from a dozen feet down the face of the cliff. He held up a silver bar.

"Damned fool," muttered Squinty.

"You want to join the other two down there?" Underwood asked sharply.

"Hell, boss, I can't see fer shit. Ain't got any sense of how far things are."

Slocum marveled that Squinty was a good shot but had no way of telling how far something was.

"If it's touchin' your fingertips, you know where it is. You know the feel of silver. I've seen you roll silver dollars around 'twixt your fingers like they was turned to liquid."

"What are you gonna do 'bout them?" Squinty said, directing Underwood's attention back to Slocum and Tamara.

"That's a question. Slocum helped out, but he let the silver get tossed into a river. It'll take the better part of a week and a couple dozen men fishin' it all out."

"You'll get it back eventually," Tamara said. "We had

172

nothing to do with Harry and Riley killing Baldy or stealing the railroad's shipment."

"You reckon what's down below is all the missing silver?" Underwood watched Slocum closely.

With a poker face and exerting every bit of control he had, Slocum said, "Yes." He left it at that. It never paid to add to a lie. Some detail always tripped up the man trying to embellish what he knew wasn't the truth.

"You agree?" Underwood trained his keen look on Tamara, who seconded Slocum's opinion. "Then there's not much more we can do here but wait for a train to take us back to the Oakland depot."

"That'll be longer than a day," Tamara said. "Two trains going to San Francisco in the same day means the next one, maybe two, will go the other direction to Sacramento."

"I'm in no hurry. We got plenny o' salvage work to do here." Underwood spat over the cliff. The gob caught the wind and rose before spiraling downward to the river. He missed the two men scouring the cliff for silver, who never noticed because they were so busy risking their lives to get just one more bar before climbing back to safety.

"Squinty, me and you'll see these folks back to a spot along the tracks to wait for the train home."

"Right, boss." The sharpshooter started to mount, but Underwood stopped him.

"On second thought, you watch them varmints down there. I wouldn't put it past either of them to toss the bars to the river so they could fetch them for themselves later."

"I'll keep an eye on them." Squinty chuckled. "Can't do more 'n that since one's all I got left." He settled on the ledge, his feet dangling over.

"We'll go back, the three of us. Don't you try anything," Underwood said.

They rode to the tracks, Underwood and Tamara chatting as if they were the best of friends. Slocum still had his six-shooter, but using it on Underwood meant shooting past the woman. Underwood cleverly kept Tamara between them to prevent such a bid for freedom.

"We pitch camp here," Underwood said. He got down, stretched mightily, and said, "I'm tuckered out. Don't you go nowhere while I take a nap. The sun's nice and warm on these old bones." He proceeded to unroll his blanket and stretch out, clutching the shotgun as if it were a lover who might sneak away.

Slocum and Tamara looked at each other. She mouthed, "What'll we do?"

Slocum showed her. He walked his horse a hundred yards up the line toward San Francisco. She joined him. They both mounted and started riding before they spoke.

"He let us go," she said.

"After a crew finds the silver lost down the cliff, he's in the catbird seat. He'll match what Deputy Ford returned."

"Jackson's is lost because he's dead," she said. Then she stared hard at Slocum. "Are you thinking what I am?"

"Drury's share is still out there. Where he hid his, being in such feeble condition, is a poser."

"He might not have been that bad off during the robbery," Tamara said, her excitement growing. "If he'd just smoked opium, he might have been as strong and alert as any of the others."

Slocum pushed the mare a little harder to start a long upward slope toward the pass. On the other side was the stretch of railroad where the robbery had occurred. And past the next summit it was all downhill into Oakland. From there taking the ferry from Berkeley to San Francisco was a matter of a few hours.

"He's gone back to San Francisco to get more opium," Tamara kept on, putting voice to what Slocum had already decided. "We can find him and get him to tell us where he hid his share. In his condition now he's too weak to move it by himself!"

"That's the way I see it," Slocum said.

It took them until noon the next day to reach San Francisco, and Slocum spent every instant looking over his shoulder, just in case.

"I wish I could ask Underwood where to find him," Tamara said. She looked around outside the line of saloons and moved closer to Slocum.

"We've only started," he told her. A saloon wasn't the place to find Drury. Most of the silver had slipped through their fingers, but the opium addict gave them their last chance to get a piece of the stolen shipment. Slocum touched the single silver bar in his pocket he had won from the man in the card game. This might end up being the only profit he saw from getting shot at and almost dying more times than he could count.

"If I go in and—"

"You wouldn't last ten seconds," he told her. "Not a woman who looks like you."

"Is that an insult?" She drew herself up and pressed her hand over the hole torn in her blouse. She had tied it together with a small knot that kept coming unfastened. Her fingers pressed into it and the softness beneath.

"Any whore along the Barbary Coast sells herself for a quarter a trick."

"That's outrageous!"

"What's really outrageous is that her pimp probably gets her doped up on laudanum or drunk off cheap rotgut and then takes the entire night's money. Maybe as much as ten dollars."

"Ten? That'd mean . . . Oh." Tamara put her hand over her mouth to stifle the outcry. "I can't expect you to take the risk of going into each saloon and asking after him."

"He's not here," Slocum said. The smell of decaying fish and the ocean gagged him. "We need to go to Chinatown."

"The opium dens," she said, nodding. "Of course. But it'll be even harder there. I don't speak Chinese, and I am sure you don't."

Slocum ignored how easily she assumed he spoke no Chinese. That she was right mattered less than finding Drury fast. The robber might have been chasing the dragon for days. A week? It all depended on when he and Baldy had parted company. Baldy had taken it into his head to retrieve his share and hightail it. Drury might have grabbed a few silver bars from his hoard and returned to San Francisco for his drugs. That was the best Slocum could hope for.

"Dupont Gai is that way," Tamara said, pointing. "I've never been there. There wasn't any reason."

"Didn't the railroad hire Chinese to lay the tracks through the mountains?"

"Yes, but Mr. Collingswood hired Celestial recruiters. I don't think even Underwood ventured into Chinatown. It's a very dangerous place."

Slocum turned his back on the Barbary Coast. Chinatown couldn't be any more dangerous, even with rumors of vicious Chinese gangs called tongs and a rabbit warren of tunnels beneath the streets to hide the opium dens and give escape routes when the police raided street-level stores.

They walked south and turned toward the east a mile from the Bay. Dupont Street was crowded with Chinese darting about on arcane business. Decapitated chickens hung by their feet in front of butcher stores and trays of greens attracted crowds, all chattering and pushing money back and forth in deals that defied logic—or any logic Slocum knew.

"How do we find a den of iniquity, John?" She clung to his arm so hard the circulation was cut off.

He steered her into a filthy alley and moved in front of her.

"How are you as an actress?"

"Why, I— Why do you want to know?"

"You're going to be an addict. I'll carry you. Maybe half drag you. I'll ask after your brother and say you want to smoke some opium with him."

"Drury," she said. "Do you think it'll work?"

"We don't have any other way of convincing an opium den owner to show us to Drury."

"There must be dozens." She inhaled deeply and sucked in what Slocum already had. The distinctive scent of burning opium seeped from the building foundations, hinting at secret subterranean dens. "Do we inquire everywhere?"

Slocum saw no better plan. He unfastened the knot holding her ripped blouse together. It flopped down and exposed her firm, conical breast. She swatted his hand as he reached to touch it. He pushed her hand away and smeared some of the grime from his hand onto it.

"Makes you a bit more decent, even when you're playing indecent."

"Why, John, don't you remember how indecent I can be? I'll have to show you exactly how indecorous I can be."

"Later. The silver first." This put her back on track. She threw her forearm up over her face and pretended to swoon.

Slocum caught her easily, then pulled her upright. It took a few steps for them to work together. When they got back into the street, he defied anyone to believe she wasn't hurting for opium.

More than an hour and six dens later, they came to a door opening onto an alley. Slocum had learned to spot the dens by the burly guards stationed outside. Many carried wickedly sharp hatchets thrust in their sashes. This one wore two butcher knives and swung a meat cleaver back and forth with a faint whistling sound.

Slocum explained what they wanted, how Tamara needed to find her brother.

The man stood as solid as a statue, arms crossed. The gleaming cleaver in his right hand warned them not to try to enter.

"Money. We have money." Slocum pulled out the silver bar and showed it. The man's eyes widened slightly, then he gave a single nod, rapped on the door, and stood back as it opened.

The rush of smoke and heat from below made Slocum as weak as Tamara pretended. The splintery stairs had been built for lighter men and sagged with every step. When they reached the bottom of the flight, the darkness almost defeated him. Smoke burned his eyes, and only a single lamp burned at the end of a long narrow corridor. He and Tamara walked down it slowly. The passage was too narrow for him to continue supporting her weight. He went ahead of her, and she shuffled along, feigning debilitating need for the drug as well as she could.

"You pay. Now," said a wizened man who hardly came to Slocum's shoulder. He was hunched over, and his thrust-out hand twitched like a bony claw.

"We're looking for her brother. They will smoke together if he is here. We will pay for more of his opium. *Ya pien,*" Slocum said, mimicking the word he had heard used by other Chinese in the hunt for Drury.

"Madak. *Ya pien* smoke with tobacco. Good. Good. Expensive." The man thrust his hand out farther.

"We must find—"

"He's here, John! Drury's here!"

Slocum took out the silver bar and placed it in the gate-keeper's hand. It disappeared into the folds of a robe that hung like a tent around a scrawny body.

Slocum knelt beside the bunk where Drury lay, his eyes open and staring sightlessly. His skin had turned to tissue paper, tightly strung over his bones. In his half-open mouth Slocum saw a blackened tongue.

"Where is it, Drury? Tell me where the silver is." Tamara shook the man. His head flopped from side to side.

Slocum pulled her back. She struggled to get free and force Drury to tell her where his portion from the robbery was hidden.

"He's dead," Slocum said harshly. "He's not going to tell us anything. From the look of him, he's been dead for a day."

"But he can't be."

Slocum swung her around bodily and pushed her back toward the man who had taken the silver. Before Slocum could demand it back, a commotion down the long hall caught his attention. Men shouted in English and rushed forward. The Chinaman tried to duck down under a table. Slocum saw the dark round hole there that would have let the man escape into the maze of tunnels under the streets. As he pulled him up on his toes, kicking and struggling, Underwood pushed past and lifted his shotgun.

The roar deafened Slocum. He fell back as the Celestial seemed to explode when the buckshot tore him apart. Slocum stared at his coat and vest covered with the man's innards and blood.

"You make quite an entry, Underwood." Slocum tried wiping the gore from his coat. His hands were quickly caked with blood and gore.

"You'da been gutted if I hadn't." Underwood bent. Using his crippled hand, he scooped up a knife with a long, razor-sharp blade. "He had it aimed right for your heart."

"I should thank you," Slocum said.

"But you're not sure you can do it," Underwood said. "Gus, you find the son of a bitch?"

"Deader 'n a mackerel, boss."

"Where's the rest of the silver, Slocum?" Underwood tapped the knife on Slocum's shoulder, then slid it closer to his throat. Slocum didn't move a muscle.

"He was dead when we got here," Tamara said. "That's the truth. Wherever he hid his share, it's still out there."

"We been scourin' the countryside and ain't found it," Underwood said. "I was hopin' you'd put me on to it—for the reward, of course."

"Of course," Slocum said sarcastically. He felt empty inside after all that had happened.

"Boss, lookee here." Gus held up the silver bar Slocum had given the opium den owner.

"Now how he'd get that?"

Slocum looked Underwood squarely in the eye and said, "Drury must have paid for his smoke with it."

Underwood looked to Tamara, who nodded.

"Reckon that's it, then. The outlaws are all dead. That son of a bitch Ford collected part of the reward for returnin' what he did to Mr. Collingswood. It'll be another week to pick up the bars that dropped down the cliff, but from what we got back so far, that's only half of the full shipment."

"What now?" Slocum asked.

Underwood snorted, tossed aside the knife, and took the bar from Gus.

"I report to Mr. Collingswood. Workin' for him ain't the best job in the world, but it's better than anything else I can do." He spun around and stalked off, Gus following him.

Slocum and Tamara stared at each other, then hastily followed. By the time they climbed the stairs and exited into the alley, Underwood was nowhere to be seen.

"It's the end of the trail," Slocum said.

Tamara clung to him, shaking with emotion. She pushed back, stared up into his green eyes, and smiled weakly.

"Not yet, John. Not quite yet."

18

"My treat, John. It's the least I can do." Tamara bowed and swept her arm out to indicate the bathhouse door.

The heat boiling from inside the stone-walled room began erasing the sweat and grime from his face and hands the instant he stepped inside. Buckets of hot water stood around a large galvanized tub with a high back. Clean towels lay on a table on the far side of the tub.

"Get out of those clothes. By the time we're through, they'll be all clean."

Slocum peeled the clothes stuck to his skin with blood and handed them to Tamara. She laid the filthy garments over the back of the tub and quickly shucked off her own clothes to stand gloriously naked. Even with dirt smeared all over her, some of it by Slocum's own hand, she was gorgeous. She swept up the pile of clothes and took them to the door, held her arm out, then pulled it back without the clothes.

"The Chinese are good at things other than building railroads or smoking opium. This bathhouse is the finest in all of San Francisco."

"Seeing you like that makes me think of something more than a bath."

"I noticed," she said, glancing at his groin. "That'll happen—in due time. Wash first, then . . . indecency later."

She herded him into the tub. The cold metal caused gooseflesh to ripple on his skin. Then he yelped when she began dumping in the hot water. He leaned back and soaked in the warmth. Closing his eyes, he began to drift. It had been too long since he'd felt this relaxed.

Then realization slipped away as Tamara joined him in the tub. She straddled his waist, facing him. Her thighs pressed into his as she began scrubbing with a soft rag and plenty of soap. She worked from his face, down his chest. The hair had become matted with the Chinaman's blood. This vanished and let her work still lower, down to his crotch, where his manhood poked above the water like a one-eyed snake.

"I want to be sure this is nice and clean . . . before we get down to the dirty deeds."

Slocum grabbed the fallen bar of soap and slathered it over her chest. Hard pink points poked through the lather. He gave those twin peaks special treatment as she worked on his shaft. Together they began thrashing about, splashing water over the rim of the tub. Tamara rose, positioned herself, and gripped him firmly.

Her eyes opened and locked with his. Then she lowered her hips and guided him into her inner fastness. Fully inside her, Slocum tried to lift himself up. His movement proved too awkward because of the way she pinned him down, and the sides of tub prevented much movement.

"I'll do it all, darling," she said. Tamara rocked back and let him slip halfway from her nether lips. "I'll do it *all*."

She began rotating her hips, moving him around although he was only half inside. Then she shoved herself down and took him fully. This time her rotary motion caused Slocum to gasp. She was tight and hot around him. The sloshing water stimulated his skin and the sight of her breasts bobbing gently as she moved thrilled him to the breaking point. He fought for control. He wanted this to last as long as Tamara could move.

He reached out and caught her tits, capturing the hard nips between thumbs and forefingers. He squeezed down gently, released them, and then mashed his palms down as she moved. She squealed with glee and began moving faster. Her knees slipped back and forth along the bottom of the tub, adding to the sensation rippling into Slocum's loins.

He slipped his soap-slick hands from her breasts, down her sides, and around to grip the double handful of her ass cheeks. Pretending they were lumps of dough, he kneaded and moved, sometimes with her body and other times against the motion. Either way caused her body to quiver and jerk with new desire for him.

She bent forward and kissed him. Lips locked, she began moving with greater urgency. She tensed around his hidden shaft, as if an invisible hand milked him. She began lifting and falling faster. He guided her with his hands gripping her behind. He stared at the rictus of pure passion on her face, then closed his eyes and lost himself to the motion, the friction, the nearness, her body . . . the totality of Tamara Crittenden.

He grunted as he exploded. Her hips went wild as if this was the touch that lit her fuse. Locked together, they crashed about in the tub and lost most of the water in it. By the time their passion was spent and they clung to each other's naked, wet bodies, Slocum knew he had received the best reward possible for all he had been through.

She pushed him back as she moved to stare at him. He tried to read her expression but couldn't.

"Time for more water and a final scrub-down," she said.

He enjoyed the sight of her rising from what water remained. Soapsuds still clung to parts of her body, but nothing exciting was hidden. She dumped the last buckets of hot water in, then joined him. This time they finished the bath and languished in the cooling water, his arms around her as she sat on his lap facing away.

"Is there any chance we can find Drury's share?"

"With Underwood and his men searching, I doubt it. He knew that Baldy and Drury were partners. They would have hidden their shares near one another."

"Oh, John, to be so close." She leaned back and ran her hands up and down the outsides of his legs. Even as she did so, all erotic message was lost. He knew her thoughts were on silver, not him.

"What are you going to do?" He stroked over her water-slickened breasts and got the response he thought he would. Nothing. She was lost in the mountains east of San Francisco, across the Bay, and along the stretch of the Central California Railroad where the robbery had occurred.

"It's time for me to leave town," she said. "Mr. Collingswood isn't likely to think well of me, and I don't want him sending Underwood after me to, well, you can guess."

"Underwood let us go twice."

"You're no fool, John. He let *me* go. You were only standing close enough to be included."

"That's how I saw it, too," he said. He sat up, urged her to stand. For a moment he stared at her delightful naked body, then he got out of the tub.

"I'll dry you off," she said, taking a towel and applying it to his flesh.

It would have been exciting if there hadn't been a "good-bye" mixed in with it. He returned the favor, and by the time they were both dry, their clothes had been returned fresh and cleaner than Slocum remembered them ever being. Even the tears and bullet holes had been mended. They dressed in silence, then took each other in their arms and kissed.

"As the French say, *au revoir*. That's not a good-bye as much as 'see you later,' " she said.

"*Hasta la vista* is the same thing, only in Spanish."

She laughed with forced gaiety and put her cheek against his chest for a moment, then pushed away.

"Aren't we the maudlin ones? It's been good, John. I wish it had been more lucrative. You even had to give up the single silver bar to get us out of that opium den."

"Underwood can use it more than I can. He'll prove his usefulness to Collingswood by handing it over. All I'd do would be use it for whiskey."

"Just whiskey? Not whiskey and women?"

"Just whiskey," he assured her.

"You are such a liar."

She smiled sadly, put her hand on his chest, moved away, and was gone. Slocum stared at the empty doorway for a while, then followed. By the time he got into the street, Tamara was nowhere to be seen. He found his mare—or the one he was stealing from the Central California Railroad as payment for all he had been through—and rode to the ferry. Every step closer to the boat added another touch of loss.

Until it occurred to him.

Slocum had ridden hard and reached the spot where Jackson's map had led before. He lined up the mountains and then settled down to see if anyone was on his back trail. All the way from San Francisco he had worried that Underwood or one of his men would be after him. There hadn't been anyone obviously interested in him. After another half hour, he stood and took a final look around. Then he fished out Jackson's treasure map.

He laid it down, positioned it according to the mountain peaks, and then remembered what Tamara had said about the robber. He got things mixed up. Simple directions got reversed. Left was right to him.

Slocum lifted the map and let the sun shine through the paper. The signal peaks changed this way so Slocum turned until they matched up once more. Instead of hunting along the trail, he saw that the map indicated a spot some distance to the right of the trail. He began walking and within twenty minutes found a series of caves.

A quick look convinced him none of them held Jackson's share of the robbery. But he remembered how little time the outlaws thought they had before a posse came after them. Slocum sat on a rock, then looked down a steep embankment. He scrambled a few feet and saw how the rocks had been dislodged. At the edge of a crevice he flopped onto his belly and looked into the dim recess. He pulled out a lucifer, struck it, and set fire to a dried clump of brush. Dropping it into the crevice brought a smile to his lips.

Silver. A flash of silver from the bottom. Jackson had dumped it down so it would be hidden from sight. But was it easily retrieved?

Slocum got his rope and tied it around a rock, then dropped the free end into the crevice. He lowered himself until he barely had room to turn. The bars of silver were stacked up knee deep. Taking off his coat, he fashioned a rude knapsack, then worked his way up to the surface to dump the bars.

All afternoon he worked to remove the stolen silver. The final trip up the rope caused his aching back to protest. His shoulders had been weighed down by more than two hundred pounds of silver, and he was filthy from rubbing against the rocky walls of the shaft.

He pulled himself up the final few feet and sat heavily. He had piled the bars neatly, but he saw one was missing.

He didn't bother reaching for his six-shooter. Instead, he asked without looking back over his shoulder, "Where are you headed?"

Tamara Crittenden stepped from a cave, holding the missing bar in her hands. She replaced it on the neat stack and then said, "Wherever you are, John."

"I have a mind to settle down."

"Do tell."

"I've been on the trail too long, and the notion of raising Appaloosas up in Oregon appeals to me, now that I have the money."

Tamara came over and stood beside him, her hand on his shoulder. She evaluated the silver bars critically.

"Half of this pile, as impressive as it is, won't buy that ranch."

"I know," he said. Their eyes locked.

"The notion of a stud farm appeals to me," she said. "If you're the stud."

Slocum laughed. She kept things light when his thoughts turned dark. He needed that brightness in his life.

"Working a horse ranch isn't easy," he said. "I know horses. I've farmed, I've done most things out West."

"But it is what you want to do." Tamara moved closer and put her arms around his shoulders before laying her cheek on his shoulder. "Do you remember what I said a long time back?"

He said nothing. His heart threatened to explode.

"I said I loved you. I'd never said that to a man before. Ever. It came out so easy and natural with you. I love you, John Slocum."

He kissed her to show he felt the same way about her. Drifting had been right for him. Until now. Until she had come along and shown him a woman could be a partner and a lover and everything he was not.

"This is your last chance to take your half of the silver," he said. Their faces were inches apart. He had never been happier when she smiled, just a little.

"We need to hit the trail. It's a long way to Oregon," Tamara said decisively.

He kissed her again to seal the deal. Horses first, then more? A family appealed to him more than it ever had since the war, especially if a boy took after his brother, Robert, and the girls their mother. But that kind of deal had to be sealed with more than a handshake or a kiss.

It took a day to load the silver and a week to reach Oregon and a month to get settled on a small ranch near Grants Pass. John Slocum had found what he had sought for so many years.

Finally.